W9-ATT-622

THE INFINITY OF
YOU & ME

THE INFINITY OF
YOU & ME

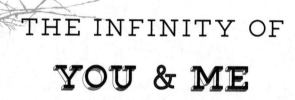

J. Q. Coyle

St. Martin's Griffin ⚏ New York

For Idil Sobel

———

THE INFINITY OF YOU & ME. Copyright © 2016 by Julianna Baggott. All rights reserved. Printed in the United States of America. For information, address St. Martin's Press, 175 Fifth Avenue, New York, N.Y. 10010.

www.stmartins.com

Library of Congress Cataloging-in-Publication Data
Names: Coyle, J. Q., author.
Title: The infinity of you & me / J. Q. Coyle.
Other titles: Infinity of you and me
Description: New York: St. Martin's Griffin, 2016.
Identifiers: LCCN 2016012740| ISBN 9781250099228 (hardcover) |
    ISBN 9781250099235 (e-book)
Subjects: LCSH: Teenage girls—Fiction. | GSAFD: Fantasy fiction.
Classification: LCC PS3552.A339 I54 2016 | DDC 813/.54—dc23
LC record available at https://lccn.loc.gov/2016012740

Our books may be purchased in bulk for promotional, educational, or business use. Please contact your local bookseller or the Macmillan Corporate and Premium Sales Department at 1-800-221-7945, extension 5442, or by e-mail at MacmillanSpecialMarkets@macmillan.com.

First Edition: November 2016

10 9 8 7 6 5 4 3 2 1

ACKNOWLEDGMENTS

The term *spandrel* was brought to our attention by the poet Frank Giampietro who, inspired by its architectural definition, created a new kind of poem which he named the spandrel. His book *Spandrel*, cocreated with Denise Bookwalter, is a beautiful work of art. We thank him for the spark.

We are deeply grateful to our early readers: Kirsten Carleton, Julie Stevenson, Olivia Ghafoerkhan, Jim Zola, Trish Tulli, Lynn York, and Heather Whitaker (editor extraordinaire). As ever we are thankful for Justin Manask and Nat Sobel—and the entire Sobel Weber team—who have been such strong advocates for this novel. Thank you, Idil Sobel, for being a great champion as well as lending an editorial eye. And thank you, Vicki Lame, our intrepid editor; we're so happy to be on this journey with you.

Your essential state is . . . a field of infinite possibilities.

—DEEPAK CHOPRA

I saw my life branching out before me like the green fig tree. . . .

—SYLVIA PLATH

PART I
SEED

CHAPTER ONE

THE BEGINNING is always a surprise.

(The endings are, too.)

I never quite know what I look like. I'm myself, yes, but different. Never tall and leggy, but my hair might be long and tied back or cut in a short bob. Sometimes I'm in jeans and sneakers. Once or twice, a dress.

I've been alone in a field of snow.

I've woken up in the backseat of a fast car at night, my father driving down a dark road.

I've been standing in the corner at a party where none of the faces are familiar.

This time, noise comes first. A clanging deep inside the hull of a ship—a cruise ship. I'm running down a corridor of soaked red carpet.

The ship lurches.

Someone's yelling over the crackling PA speakers—I can't understand the words over the rush of water. Alarms roar overhead.

I shoulder my way down another corridor, fighting the flood of people running in the opposite direction, screaming to each other.

Some part of my brain says, *Me? On a cruise ship? Never.* But if I was so lucky, it'd be a sinking one.

The rest of my brain is sure this isn't real, no matter how real it feels.

I run my hand down the wall, the cold water now pushing against my legs. I'm wearing a pair of skinny jeans I don't own. I know someone's after me—I just don't know who. I look back over my shoulder, trying to see if anyone else is moving against the crowd like I am.

No one is.

Where's my mother? She's never here when I go off in my head like this.

A man grabs me roughly by the shirt. My ribs tighten.

Is this who I'm running from?

No. He's old, his eyes bloodshot and wild with fear. He says something in Russian, like the guys in the deli at Berezka's, not too far from my house in Southie. I shouldn't be able to understand him, but I do. *"Run! This way. Do you want to die, girl?"* I don't speak Russian. I'm failing Spanish II.

But then I answer, partly in Russian. "I'm fine. Thank you. *Spasiba.*" The words feel stiff in my mouth. I can barely hear myself over the screaming, the water rushing up the corridor, and the groaning ship.

The man keeps yelling, won't let go of me, so I rip myself loose and run.

A glimpse of gray through a porthole, only a sliver of land and heavy dark sky.

I see myself in the porthole's dark reflection—my hair chin length, my bangs choppy, just a bit of faded red lipstick.

We're on the Dnieper River. It's like this: I know things I shouldn't. I don't know how.

A woman falls. I reach down and help her up. Her head is gashed, her face smeared with blood. She nods a thank-you and keeps marching against the current, soaked.

I wonder if she'll make it. Will I?

I'm looking for my father. I want to call out for him, but I shouldn't. The people chasing me are really after him—I know this too, the way you know things in a dream.

The ship lists, hard, and my right shoulder drives into a wall. Stateroom doors swing open. The sound of water surging into the hull is impossibly loud.

And then my father appears up ahead—shaggy, unshaven, his knuckles bloody. I love seeing him in these hallucinations. (That's what my therapist calls them.) It's the only time I ever see him. I even love seeing him when he looks like hell, and older than I remember him, more worn-down. But he always has this energy—like his strength is coiled and tensed.

"Alicia!" he shouts. "Down!"

I fall to my knees. The water is up to my neck and so cold it shocks my bones.

My father raises a gun and fires.

Some men fire back.

I put my head underwater, and the world is muted. I hold my breath, can only hear my heart pounding in my ears. My face burns with the cold, my back tight, lungs pinched. I swim toward the blurry yellow glow of an emergency light.

When I lift my head, a tall and angular man slides down a wall and goes under, leaving a swirl of blood. My father shot him. This should shock me, but it doesn't. My father, who's really a stranger to me, is always on the run and often armed.

Another man, thick necked and yelling, returns fire from a cabin doorway.

My father disappears around the corner up ahead, then lays cover for me. "Get up!" he shouts. "Move now!"

I push through the icy water, wishing my legs were stronger and tougher, feeling small and easily kicked off-balance.

"Just up ahead," he says, "—stairs."

But then a little boy with a buzz cut doggy-paddles out of a cabin. The water's too deep for him.

I reach out, and he grabs my hand, clinging to my shirt.

"Alicia, get down!" my father yells.

Instinctively, I shield the kid.

A gunshot.

I feel a shattering jolt in my shoulder blade. I can't breathe, can't scream.

The boy cries out, but he hasn't been shot. I have. The pain is stabbing. "He shot me!" I shout, shocked. I can only state the obvious, my voice so rough and ragged I don't even recognize it.

My father pulls me and the boy into a tight circular stairwell, the water whirling around us, chest deep. As he lifts the little boy high up the stairs, I glimpse the edge of a tattoo and skin rough with small dark scars and fresh nicks on his wrists. "Keep climbing!" he says to the little boy.

Wide-eyed with fear, the boy does what he's told.

The water is rising up the stairs, fast, but my father props me up with his shoulder, and we keep climbing. I try to remember what it was like before he left my mom and me. Did he carry me to bed, up the stairs, down the hallway, and tuck me in?

"We're going to get out," my father says. "We can jump."

"We can't jump," I say. Off the ship?

"Trust me," my father says.

I've never trusted my father, never had the chance. After he left, he wasn't allowed within five hundred feet of me or my mother. "What the hell am I doing here?" I ask.

My father stares at me. "Is it you? Really *you*?"

"Yes, it's me," I say. Of course it's me!

My father looks stunned and scared and relieved somehow all at the same time. "You're finally here."

"Finally where?"

"Things have gotten too dangerous," he says quickly. He reaches into his pocket, and in his hand I glimpse what looks like a strangely shaped shiny wooden cross about the width of his palm, but it's not a cross, not exactly. "You've got to get lost and stay lost."

I am lost, I want to tell him, but the pain in my back is so sharp it takes my breath.

As the water pushes us up the stairwell, my blood swirls around me like a cape. I can't die here.

I look up into cloudy daylight.

The ship's listing so hard now it seems to be jackknifing. Suddenly I'm terrified we're all going to drown.

I expect to see the little boy's face at the top of the stairs, but he's gone. Instead, there's a group of men with guns trained on my father and me.

"Ellington Maxwell." The man who speaks is the one who shot me. In the hazy glare off the water I see a jagged scar on his cheek. "Welcome to our world. This time we hope you stay awhile."

I look up at the sky again and abruptly it swells with sun. My right hand hurts and I know this signals an ending . . . Bright, blazing, obliterating light.

And I'm gone.

CHAPTER TWO

OVERHEAD, THE greenish glow of buzzing fluorescent lights.

I'm back.

In Spanish class.

I'm sitting at the same desk where I was before the last flash came on. The room is quiet. Everyone else is bent over their desks.

We're taking a test. My name, Alicia Maxwell, is written in the top right-hand corner of the page, except that, for a minute, it doesn't look like my name, like when you look at a word over and over again until it doesn't seem to spell anything. Next to it is one of my tree doodles. Not just the trunk and branches, but also the roots, a mirror image. Sometimes I catch myself drawing different versions of that tree, even when I'm not flashing.

How long have I been out of it? I look at the cracked plastic clock, but it's about four hours off. It stopped ticking months ago.

Señor Fernandez catches my eye and gives a close-lipped smile. He knows I'm flunking this test. He probably knows I'm flunking my entire sophomore year.

I look down at the paper. Multiple choice—that's what set me off. Making decisions, even small ones, can knock me out of my-self. I'm allowed to get out of multiple-choice tests, and Fernandez said I could take an essay test, but I'm not that great at Spanish, so I opted for something with better odds.

Except I'd gotten so nervous, I was chewing my nails and I ripped a small bit of skin next to my fingernail. I tore off a corner of the test to stop the bleeding. It bloomed red, seeping into the paper, and my neck ached, the pressure building in my chest so much that it felt like it could rip in half—the hallucination coming on. My desk felt wobbly, the room shook and seemed to crack, letting in seams of darkness. And then this world fell away, another one appearing in its place—even if just in my own demented head.

When I'm hallucinating, I kind of keep going in this world. I stare at my test and there's the proof. I finished it, guessing all the way, but I have no real memory of it.

I think of Sylvia Plath, and I almost hear her voice, her poem about shutting your eyes and the world dropping dead, then open-ing them to find that everything's born anew. I'm pretty sure I'm crazy, so it makes sense that one of my favorite poems is called "Mad Girl's Love Song."

That pain in my right hand, it's always the same. It means I'm about to get thrown back into my own life, Spanish failures and all.

The bell whines, and Señor Fernandez goes to the door to col-lect the tests as we head out.

I shrug at my paper, apologizing to it personally. I pull on my backpack, walk up to Señor Fernandez, and hand it in.

"You get hungry?" he asks, pointing out the missing corner.

"*Siempre tengo muchos hambre?*" I say, which might mean that I'm always very hungry. And I am, but not in the food way. I'm hun-gry for something that I've got no name for, something in those hallucinations—a fear but also an ache and I don't know how to get it to ease up. Or even if I want to.

Hafeez is waiting for me in the hall. He's all elbows and knees, all hinges and odd angles—too tall for his own good. He pats down his thick dark hair like he always does, embarrassed about its lumpiness. His older sister gives him haircuts—she's no pro. (Not that I have room to talk. I'm kind of a jeans and T-shirt type, not much makeup except for eyeliner, my brown hair always a little messy.)

Hafeez is my best friend. Correction: my only friend.

I fight my way through the crowded hallway to get close enough to hear him over the shouting and lockers clanging and whatnot. "What happened in there?" he asks.

As we head toward the cafeteria, I tell him about the latest hallucination. I like to get them off my chest, and Hafeez is the only person I can confide in—besides my therapist, Jane, who I *half*-confide in.

When I'm done, Hafeez shakes his head. "Your mind is one dark and twisted place."

This school feels like a dark and twisted place to me. But I can't deny that Hafeez is right. "You know how cartoons show hamsters running on little wheels in their heads? It's like my hamster's dropping acid."

"Hey, at least *you're* not dropping acid," Hafeez says, pointing to some burnouts duct-taping themselves to a water fountain.

"What's the youth of America coming to, Hafeez?" We have a habit of commenting on today's youth to make us feel a little removed. It makes us feel better.

"Hell if I know. I'm looking for a loophole."

"To what?"

"Um, away from all this?" he says, waving his hand in the air. "You know what my birthday wish was this year?"

"Didn't you just turn sixteen?" Hafeez is a junior. He was nice to me last year when I was a lowly freshman, and he really didn't have to be. Sometimes I think he might have a crush on me, but he'd never admit it. I wouldn't know what to do if he did. I just want to be friends, but I wonder sometimes, if he caught me at just the right moment, could it be different? But it doesn't matter. I don't want to risk what we have. I need him too much. "Aren't you a little old for birthday wishes?"

"To fast-forward to when I own a car."

I nod but I don't want to fast-forward. I'm scared of the future. Sometimes I think there's something inside of me that wants out. I feel like this thing has its own heat and no one can see it, but if they could, they'd be looking at a kid burning up, from the inside out.

The burning up has a diagnosis—in fact, lots of them. Jane has me pegged with ADD, ADHD, anxiety/depression, paranoia, hallucinations, a dissociative disorder, and paralyzing indecision. I've even made it onto the autism spectrum. I've looked up hallucinations—all kinds, even the ones that blind people have. "Perceptions without stimuli" they're called. I might be schizo or psychotic, or the neurons in my brain are shot. My mom says, "You get tired. That's all. You just get overtired." Like this could all be fixed if I took more naps.

"What if it's already too late for me?" I stop and look down the hall. All those kids—all their neurons firing away like firecrackers. "What if I'm already a junkie?"

Hafeez stops, then snorts out a laugh. "All those pills you got in that plastic days-of-the-week container? I think little old ladies in Boca Raton work like that—not junkies," he says. He's trying to make me feel better, but it doesn't work.

I'm not addicted to pills. I'm addicted to disappearing into my hallucinations. I hate them because they make me feel weak and out of control, but I crave them, too. My issues revved up when I hit a growth spurt a couple years ago. For a long time, there weren't any hallucinations. I just faded to black with pinholes of bright light like stars and then darkness tinged blue, some fabric of the sky. Then, one day, I could see a blade of grass edging up from dirt. I wasn't looking at it like a picture. I was *in* the picture. And then I started seeing—entering—other scenes. Not scenes. Places. And the way there can be so many rooms in a house, I kept finding doors opening to rooms with more doors.

"The whole thing lasted longer this time," I tell Hafeez as we're pushed along by the crowd. "Usually they're like YouTube on speed. I flash from one scene to the next." I call them flashes, because that's how they feel—fast and searing, but not in a good way. More like cigarette burns. "But this time, I was on a sinking cruise ship with my dad. I could feel the freezing water. I got shot." I reach to touch my shoulder blade, and of course there's nothing.

"Shot? That's new," Hafeez says. "How's your father doing these days?"

"How the hell should I know?" I'm not pissed about it. I mean, I am, but it's pretty buried. I haven't seen him, at least in real life, since I was three years old. There was a restraining order at some point that he must have taken seriously because he took off and never came back. I'll never forgive him for it, but I guess I'll never have to, because I'll most likely never see him again.

"There was a cruise ship that went down not too long ago," Hafeez says. He keeps up on world events more than most adults do. "I mean, not that it matters. Who cares if you dream about disasters that already happened?"

"They aren't dreams." I lower my voice. "You've seen me. My eyes are wide open. I keep going."

"Yeah, but you're dazed. It's like you're seventeen percent zombie." Hafeez stops at his locker to put his books away, get his lunch money, and comb his hair. I step over the legs of a girl sitting on the floor, picking at a row of long thin scabs—too precise not to have been done on purpose. She's a big girl, and her wrists are ringed like a baby's. I want to tell her that it's a crap world, like I can apologize for it or something, and that this is as real and unreal as any other bullshit existence. As the blood beads up on one of the scabs, it reminds me of my own blood, swirling in the water taken on by the ship. I'm dizzy, like I might flash again. I look away and the feeling fades.

Hafeez slams his locker, and we walk into the cafeteria. It smells like cabbage and something sickly sweet. It's a riot of noise and lights and faces, people hooting and scuffling.

We slide trays down the railings, which remind me of the metal bars on the ship deck. I try not to pick at the dark red clot on my cuticle. The memory of the pain in my shoulder tingles under my skin.

"You up for this?" Hafeez asks. The lunch line is a bad place for me. It's jammed with decisions to make—chicken or fish, pizza or pasta, side dish of green beans or not, roll? Yes or no? *Relentless.*

"I'm hungry enough," I say.

"You *sure* you're not going to lose it? Really sure?" Hafeez looks concerned.

"I never have flashes twice in one day," I say, and then add quietly, "never full-blown ones. Plus, Jane told me that I shouldn't avoid decision-making situations. I've got to face them."

"The pills are nice, too, I bet," Hafeez says, raising his eyebrows.

"They take the edge off." The truth is that they never fight off a hallucination. The flashes used to come every few months, then every few weeks, but they were blurred and dreamy. Now they're almost daily and fuller and clearer and more detailed, as if I dreamed up the places, but only remembered them through a thick mist, a fog, but now I can finally see them. They're vivid and more realistic. It feels like something is being worn away and that these hallucinations are breaking through, like radio stations emerging from static on a back road the closer you get to civilization; like if I could just get there, insanity might be a place that made sense, where the signals were actually clear.

I keep this stuff to myself.

Twice, my mother sent me to some support group for messed-up kids. We met at the community center between ballroom dancing and karate classes. One of the other kids in the group pulled a knife on me in the bathroom and stole my iPod, so I begged off— not because I was scared or pissed that I'd lost the iPod, but because I had this weird sudden desire to lean into the knife, end it all right there.

"You know where people are most likely to have a breakdown?" I say. "I've looked it up."

"I bet you have."

"Grocery stores—either the shampoo or the cereal aisles." I can feel the lunch lady's eyes on me. She's old, but her hands—in their clear plastic gloves—are big and muscular. And she has this scar across her jugular. Her name is Ruth, and she hates me. I keep talking to calm myself. "Because there are too many options in grocery stores. People crack. Grocery stores have employees trained to deal with mental breakdowns. Those people who are reshelving? They're not just reshelving. They're looking for people on the verge."

"That's probably not true." Hafeez has a very deliberate way of pronouncing his words. There's an accent in there, too, but mainly it's his very crisp way of speaking that makes him sound important, thoughtful—like he cares. And most of the time, he does, which makes him different than most of the people I know.

"But it *could* be true," I tell him.

And then Ruth starts tapping her ladle on the metal bins and running through all of the options. Gravy or not? Green beans? Chicken or fish? I can't answer. My life reduces to this one crucial moment, and pressure expands my chest.

"Stay calm," Hafeez says.

A fly spins near Ruth's face; her mouth is moving. The fly's wings are frail and frantic. I'm losing it, I'm slipping. My heart's getting louder. Do I want gravy? I hear my own voice in my head: *Stop being so stupid. Just order something!*

Ruth raises her voice: "You're holding up the line! Do I have to get Coach?" Coach is striding around with her pregnant bowling-ball belly.

"No, I got this!" I fish in my pocket for a bottle of anti-anxiety pills.

"Next!" Ruth calls, and others start to order. I'm loosening the cap when I get shoved in the back.

"Little Miss Alicia." I know the voice before I look up. Brian Sprowitz. I turn reluctantly. Sprowitz's eyes are sharp and glinty, a little hollowed out. He rubs his pale chin with his knuckles—red and chapped from the cold. "How about you hurry up?" He grinds his teeth like a speed freak. I see his friends in line behind him. All of them are on the Freaks Track, an angry crew. Most of them have had done a stint in juvie, or so the stories go. Someone once made a banner for them that said: WELCOME TO THE FUTURE BOTTOMFEEDERS OF AMERICA. On their whiteboard, people write things like: *Where Education Comes to Die* and *All the Children Left Behind*. Or maybe they write it themselves. Who knows? They're usually shadowed by a big dude in khakis who's in charge of making sure they don't hurt anyone. I don't see the big dude.

"Just go around," I say, trying to breathe normally over the pain in my chest.

In his slight accent, Hafeez tries to be disarming. "She's got this condition that affects her ability to make choices. . . ."

I shake my head. *No, Hafeez. Jesus!*

Sprowitz's eyebrows shoot up. "You want to go, Al-Qaeda?" Hafeez is called a terrorist almost every day, even though his parents left Pakistan twenty years ago and he was born in the same hospital as most of us here.

Hafeez lifts his hands, and I don't blame him.

Sprowitz walks up close to me. He moved in across the street from me two years ago, into a house with insulation-sealed windows, a place where lots of foster kids come and go. He whispers, "I know all about Alicia and her little secrets."

That I'm kind of a junkie and crazy like my father? "You don't know shit about me," I say, but my voice sounds weak. Pain shoots through my lower ribs—the short ones at the end of the rung, like someone's boring holes through them.

"Just leave her alone, please," Hafeez says, too polite to sound even remotely tough.

Sprowitz ignores him and takes a step closer to me. "Too bad about the Butlers' dog," Sprowitz says to me, and I know who he's talking about—Mr. and Mrs. Butler's dog, Arnie. He came home one night just last week, dragging his leg. It was so pulverized the vet amputated.

"What about Arnie?"

"I couldn't take it yapping in the backyard like that, and I stole a bat from the batting cages, so . . ."

I can barely breathe, barely see. "You're sick," I say, but then I immediately realize he *is* sick, that awful things must have happened to him as a kid to make him this way. I feel sorry for him all of a sudden, and then I kind of hate myself for it.

Sprowitz whispers, "I know it's just you and your hot mom in that house."

I shake my head. I'm trying to stay on my feet, trying to turn my face away from Sprowitz's sour breath.

Sprowitz slaps the pill bottle out of my hands. It smacks on the floor and rolls to the wall and stops.

Hafeez moves to pick it up but Sprowitz stops him with a look. He turns back to me and, for a second, he looks tired. Maybe he's tired of being Sprowitz but feels like he's locked in. I know the feeling. "Do you want me to fuck you up or your towelhead bitch?" he says. "How you like those choices?"

I don't like those choices at all. In fact, I've stopped breathing. My heart's seized.

I know Hafeez wants to bolt, but to his credit he stays.

Then I hear Ruth yelling for Coach again. Her gravelly voice swings louder and then muffles in my ears.

I wish I had a real father who would teach me how to get bullies to back down. I grab my own shirt, as if this will keep my chest from exploding. I feel this pressurized fear. It's like some dark shadow on a lung that's absolutely cancer. I'm afraid I could burst open, burn shit down around me. I'm more scared of myself than Sprowitz.

I look over at Hafeez, who's terrified. He knows what happens when a guy like Sprowitz gets you in his sights.

"Who am I gonna fuck up? You gonna pick or what?" Sprowitz says.

"Me," Hafeez says. "Okay? Fuck me up. How's that for a decision?"

I shake my head at Hafeez—I want to say no but I can't speak. He's already wincing, so I know the punch is coming.

He turns away but Sprowitz's fist connects anyway. Hafeez's head snaps back, and I lose my balance almost as if in sympathy for him. I grab one of the silver rails where our trays still sit, but I end up on the ground next to Hafeez, who's on his knees, hands over his face.

Sprowitz stands over us. "How was that?" he asks, and he looks like he's ready to do more, but for some reason, I can picture him as a little boy, just a scared kid trying to look tough.

I hear Coach's whistle. Boots and sneakers scuffle around us. Hafeez's lip is split and bleeding.

Coach is shouting, "Brian Sprowitz! Over here! Now!"

"You're bleeding," I tell Hafeez.

He touches his lip and his fingers come away bloody. "I'm fine," he says, but I can see tears in his eyes, and this is where I wish I could make a comment about the state of today's youth, but then I feel a series of pains pulsing all over my body, starting in this strangely familiar pattern—my collarbone, the back of my neck, my arm.

"Alicia?" Hafeez says, and I realize he knows what's happening. He grabs my arm. "Alicia, don't." But I'm feeling dizzier—the blood on his face, his grip, as if he could hold me in place, the bone-deep pain. The pain zeros in on my upper arm, a pain so deep there's no way to get at it. My heavy head jags to one side.

The cafeteria noise dims. My vision reduces to a narrow tunnel, a single beam, a small white dot.

And then I'm fading out.

My brain lights up, and the hallucinations are there, pressing at the edges. I say deep inside myself, *Go ahead. Take me out. Go on . . .*

. . . And there, in my face, is an ancient bulldog, panting. Its jaw juts out with a bank of crooked teeth.

I'm lying on the floor of an apartment. I sit up.

As my eyes adjust to the darkness, I see an old man in a rocking chair. The room is nearly empty. In fact, it looks like it's been looted.

The bulldog stares at me and whines. I pet him, my hand sliding down his knotted backbone. An undeniably real backbone.

The old man says, "You think they won't rise up here too? Fat cats left us nothing. This is class warfare, honey." It feels like part of a long muttered speech. He pulls a flask from his pants pocket, unscrews the lid, and takes a swig, then rests it for a moment on his hardened belly. He has soft jowls, shiny blue eyes, and a few light tufts of gray hair.

I wish I could see what I look like in this hallucination. But then I concentrate and I know what I look like—shorn hair, pale arms, too skinny. Suddenly, I remember the old man's name. Gemmy. What kind of a name is Gemmy? "Where's my father?" I ask.

"They got him. You know that." Gemmy screws the lid back on the flask, then, thinking better of it, unscrews it again and takes another sip.

I'm straining to remember other things. My thoughts are just out of reach.

"And here we are—sitting ducks." Gemmy shakes his head.

I get up and walk to the window. One pane is cracked. Cops on the street below are pulling over cars. The air feels alive with a buzzing noise. A flash of metal glides by the window, the size of a hummingbird. It zips off before I can get a good look.

Where the hell am I? I feel lost and disoriented. It's terrifying not to recognize where you are. I know I'm in the United States—I can see battered green highway signs. In the distance, smoke billows from what must be massive fires. I reach my hand toward the splintered window, like I expect to feel the heat. Pain shoots through my collarbone.

An image from a Plath poem appears in my brain. It's about a window that's brightening with light and then swallowing stars.

My vision fogs and blurs, is swallowed whole. . . .

. . . My hand is still pressed to a window, but I'm not looking down on a city street. Instead there's a ruined courtyard, a cityscape beyond, flickering as if behind some kind of gauze, like it's there and not there at the same time.

I turn around. The old man and the bulldog are gone. I'm in a bedroom with a rumpled queen-size bed, posters for bands I don't like, the stereo with speakers as wide as doors. In the mirror above my dresser I see myself—bleached hair, dark roots coming in, a black shirt, and expensive sneakers.

I know that this is my room and that in other rooms in this house there are thick carpets, tall slanting ceilings, heavy drapes. Beautiful, but it's all falling apart—cracks in the walls as if it's a problem deep down in the foundation.

I'm not a prisoner here but it's not safe to leave. I'm full of fear, the kind that never really goes away because it's burrowed down so deep.

I look through the large windows. Below, in the ghost-glow of an emergency light clamped to a flagpole, I see a drained, cracked pool, a moss-veined wall, and beyond it, a hulking black Humvee— the glint of a cannon-size gun barrel mounted on its side.

Two guards stand beside it.

And then I spot a boy, around my age, climbing over the courtyard wall. He's lean and quick, his shaggy dark hair gleaming.

The wall is crumbling, and a long dark scar runs across the back-yard, as if the earth itself has cracked. I've never hallucinated any-place quite like this one. It's cast in a different kind of light, brighter with darker shadows. The air is filled with static, a low hum, like a hive. Some part of it is buzzing deep down in its core.

On the other side of the wall, barren, dirt-packed land leads to what looks like a trailer park surrounded by a chain-link fence. Then the boy turns and looks up, straight at me. He has a square jaw and a handsome face, but it's too thin—he looks hungry and tired. There's a streak of dirt on his forehead and on one cheekbone. I feel some strange connection to him, an electrical current snapping between us. It's not good or bad, just strange; he's setting off some kind of alarm inside of me, but I don't know what the emergency is—fire, earthquake, terrorist attack? I feel a rush of adrenaline.

He's daring me to do something or say something. His eyes are a bright-water crystal blue.

I open the window to call to him, but he shakes his head and starts walking off.

I hear the Humvee's radio, an announcer's voice saying some-thing about martial law in Miami. What is happening to this place?

I have to tell him something—what, I don't know. I run to my bedroom door, pull it open.

Then I hear a cough somewhere down the hall. It's my mother. And I know immediately that, in this disintegrating house, she's sick. She's *very* sick. I can't save her. I know this has been true for a long time. I feel panicky, helpless. I hate this world as much as I love something about it. It's surreal, damaged, maybe even doomed.

I run the length of the hall, down the stairs to the back of the house. I open a back door. The air is hot and stale.

A guard opens the door to the Humvee and stands on the chrome running board. "Hey! Get inside!"

"I'm not a prisoner, am I?"

Am I?

The guard thinks about it and then gives a nod. "Not back in five, I sound the alarm."

I sprint across the courtyard, climb the wall, jump to the ground. I'm ready to keep running, but the boy hasn't gone far. He hears me running and turns to face me.

I'm not a stranger to him, but we aren't friends, either. He's waiting for me to say something, maybe explain myself.

He looks out across the blanched landscape. "Your father's wrong. It's not too late."

Too late for what? The dry wind whips at our faces. I wish I could help. I don't know anything except that I want this hallucination—this nightmare?—to last. This world has a hold on me. It's uglier and more beautiful than anyplace I've ever seen.

"You know if something doesn't give, it's over," he says. "Someone's explained this to you, haven't they?"

"What's over?"

He rolls his eyes, disgusted with me, and he starts talking, but I can't hear him. Everything's gone silent. I can still see his lips moving, his bright teeth. He's talking quickly, urgently.

But then everything is bright, like an extra sun has bounced into the sky. It's blinding. I feel the searing pain in my shoulder again, but also my neck, and I know I'm moving on.

And it's that sudden—he's gone.

I'm gone.

Windblown . . .

. . . Surrounded by water.

Deep pain coursing through my shoulder blade.

I'm with my father. This time we're shoved down in the back of an old speedboat, hands duct-taped behind our backs, a freezing wind going right through my shirt, which is blood-soaked from the gunshot wound, drilled into my shoulder blade.

The cold is so sharp the pain seems to be fading—everything is going numb. My ribs feel like they're cinched too tightly. My body is shaking.

The men from the cruise ship are only a few feet away, arguing over a GPS, cradling their guns loosely. The motor is loud. They must have moved us from the cruise ship to this speedboat as hostages of some sort.

My father has found a ridge in the rusted hull and is sawing at the duct tape around his wrists. I don't say a word. My father rips through the last bit of the duct tape. He pushes up the sleeve of his jacket revealing the raw skin of his inner arm scrawled with the curled edge of a tattoo. He presses hard where the tattoo curls near his wrist. He cups my face with one hand, and says, "Go back! For now, go back!"

The speedboat starts to shudder and vibrate. I try to keep my eyes open—the boat is shaking apart; we're going to drown after all or get shredded in the motor—but the gunmen don't reach out to steady themselves. It's not the boat trembling. It's my own vision of the boat, the river, the shoreline studded with houses, people on the river's edge walking along the roads in bulky hazmat suits.

My father grabs my arm. "Go, Alicia!"

My right hand hurts. I know that the hallucinations are coming to an end. . . . There's a blast of wind so cold it takes my breath. I throw my head back. Can you drown in air? I'm gasping . . .

. . . I'm on the cafeteria floor, near the legs of one of the tables. Hafeez is shaking me like he's trying to wake me. "Alicia!"

I'm not wet, not shot, but I'm shivering. The chill is deep in my bones.

I look for Sprowitz but don't see him. Did Coach haul him off? "I'm okay. Let's get out of here," I say.

"Coach told us not to move. She's coming back for us. She's really pissed." Hafeez looks pretty shaken up, the blood already crusting on his lip.

"I was with my dad again and I saw this boy," I say, more to myself than to him.

And, true to her word, Coach is marching toward us.

"You've got to look up that cruise ship," I mutter to Hafeez, my voice hoarse. "Was it on the Dnieper River?"

"Who gives a shit about that now?" he says, dabbing at his lip.

"My phone is crap, Hafeez. Can you please look it up?"

He pulls out his phone.

There are Coach's duck-footed Champion sneakers.

I look up.

Coach's whistle is resting on her pregnant belly. "I heard from a little bird that you might have something to do with starting this fight. I think Principal Waybourne would like to see you first, Hafeez. "

"It was Sprowitz!" Hafeez says.

"He says it was you two. You say it was him. All three of you have to take a stroll. Hafeez, principal's office. Alicia, you come with me."

I try to stand, my shoulder still aching from the memory of pain. One of my knees buckles, but I keep my balance.

"We really didn't start this!" Hafeez says, and Coach rolls her eyes.

"Don't," I say to Hafeez. "Just let it go." There's no fighting Coach.

I straighten up and let Coach lead me out.

But just as we get to the heavy doors, Hafeez shouts out, "That cruise ship didn't sink in the Dnieper! It was the Volga! The Volga!"

Coach whips around. "Don't get smart with me, Hafeez! Watch your mouth or you're next!"

"Volga," Hafeez says. "I said Volga."

Is the Dnieper even a real river? Or did my brain make that up, too?

CHAPTER THREE

COACH TAKES me to her office in the girls' locker room. The air is heavy with the smell of sweat and aerosol hair spray. Every time I smell it what comes to me is shame—the red ring from the waistband of my elastic underwear on my stomach as I hunched over to change into shorts and a T-shirt freshman year, and how the little metal door didn't provide much to hide behind.

"What are we doing here?"

Coach unlocks the door, pushes it open, and there's her small office with filing cabinets, an old wooden desk stacked with clipboards, and a leather chair on wheels. Nets filled with basketballs and volleyballs hang from wall hooks. It smells like Band-Aids.

"Want to tell me what happened?" Coach plops down in her seat.

"Sprowitz punched Hafeez. That's it."

Coach looks at me for a long moment then starts stacking the clipboards. "Look, Alicia. I know you're struggling. We all got the memo. But if you want good things to happen to you, you've got to think positive." She taps her head.

"Was there an actual memo?"

Coach rolls her eyes. "You've got to change your mind-set."

"So, what's happening to me—it's just a phase or something?" Coach cradles her belly, and I wonder if she's hoping her kid doesn't turn out like me. "And if I just think happy thoughts, I'll be fine?"

Coach stacks a few more clipboards, leans back in her chair, and tilts her head. "Maybe it is a phase. You should look for good opportunities instead of bad ones. Be ready, you know, to move on to other things. Just be positive. If you look for the good, it has a way of finding you." She makes it sound so simple. She pulls out a pink pass form and scribbles something on it. I think she's going to send me back to class, but then she tells me my mother's been called. "About how long does it usually take her to get here, thirty minutes or so?"

My heart squeezes. My mother has enough to deal with, being a single parent and working all the time, without me causing her more grief.

"Why'd she get called?" I ask Coach. "I didn't do anything; I'm serious. Wait. There was an actual memo, wasn't there?"

Coach looks up at me. "She's worried about you. We all are."

I want to cry, not just because I know she's right, but also because she's trying to help in her own gruff way. I feel guilty that she's even making the effort.

She hands me the pass. It has my name and her signature, but it doesn't have a destination on it. "Where am I supposed to go?"

Coach gives me a level look. "You decide, Alicia. You have thirty minutes. Then you need to go to the principal's office to meet your mom."

I stand up, still shaky from the cafeteria ordeal. I have to bite the inside of my cheek to keep from losing it. I take the pass and turn to leave.

"Remember, Alicia," Coach says. "Look for the good. Be positive."

"I'll try." I pull her door shut behind me.

I decide to head to the library—the only quiet place in the whole building. Even after my father telling me that I had to get lost and stay lost, and the gunshot wound, and all of that, it's the boy's face in that scarred world that stays in my head, his bright blue eyes. And that world—the gash in the earth, the weird deep hum at its core, its harsh light. I can't shake any of it, even though it's just a product of my malfunctioning brain.

Get lost and stay lost? Isn't that what my father's good at—staying lost? Wasn't he just asking me to be more like him?

I open the library's heavy doors.

It's quiet and empty, no one even manning the reference desk. The air is dusty and stale but comforting, like being inside a book.

I angle down the poetry aisle—the only one I've ever spent much time in—and grab the copy of Sylvia Plath's *Collected Poems*. I don't even like to tell people I love her poems, because it will absolutely make me seem like an emo girl who likes the poet who killed herself. It's not the way she died. It's the way she seems to be so alive. It's the way she seems to be talking *to me*.

I take the book and slide into a carrel. "Daddy" is the poem I always turn to, and the book knows this: it always opens to that page, talking about his "brute heart."

Is my father a brute?

A couple years ago, when the pinholes of light broke through the darkness in my hallucinations, I realized the pinholes weren't light stabbing through a fabric, but stars, part of the night sky. I should say part of *a* night sky because it wasn't *this* night sky or the one I would call *our* night sky. That's when I started scratching out poems or parts of poems. What did I know about poetry except what seemed to be cracking open in my own head? Jane told me writing would help. "Keep writing. Keep filling those notebooks," she said.

Eventually, one of the hallucinations of the night sky turned into day, and there was sunlight. I remember watching that blade of grass push its way up from dirt in fast motion. It wasn't there and then it was.

I remember the exact blade of grass, how the dirt clung to it.

After that, one world after another built itself—stitched itself together. Bark rippled around trees, leaves flipped open, buildings piled up brick by brick, suspension bridges spanned rivers with their steel cables spun like spiderwebs, and finally, details—church bells rang on the hour, plastic bags swirled in gutters, dogs pulled on their leashes, and the leashes were held on to by people.

Those were the final details, the people.

And in each world, there was some other version of myself. Another me, like this me but not quite. This is what it feels like to be known, to see a glimpse of yourself in someone else—like a winter hive, iced over, is thawing, like hibernating bees are moving their thin wings again, like being told you're still alive.

I started reading poems like crazy because they made sense when nothing else did. I tripped across Plath's poems, and it was like she was speaking a secret language. I memorized the ones that felt like confessions most of all, like when she writes about being scared of the "dark thing that sleeps" inside of her. The poem unwinds like a spool of thread as she describes the thing as "soft" and "feathery," turning within her.

My mother thinks it's not a good idea to read the work of someone who committed suicide. As if the poems would infect me.

They already have.

When the bell rings, I can hear the halls flooding with noise from the cool calm of the library. I slip the book back onto the shelf and head for the office. I have my own copy at home, under my pillow. It's dog-eared and scribbled in, with notes to myself and many of my doodles of trees with spiraling roots and branches.

I wonder what's happened to Hafeez. I could text him, but he's careful to keep his phone turned off in school. He follows rules, not just because he's a good guy, but because he thinks they might protect him in some way. Hell of a lot of good they did him today.

Time's up.

The principal's secretary, Shirl Boswell, smiles when I come in. She likes me, but it makes me sad that she's so used to seeing me show up here. I get sent by teachers for just fading out and not respond-ing when they ask me questions. I get sent in because sometimes I fade out and other kids take that moment to want to talk to me. Then, of course, there are the couple of times I'm kind of ignoring them, more or less—not all there—and they've gotten pissed and suddenly I'm back in the real world in a fight. In other words, Shirl Boswell and I know each other pretty well.

"Have you ever heard of a river called the Volga, Shirl?"

She gives me a warning look for using her first name, then shakes her head. "I vacation on the Cape." Then she softens. "You okay? Tough day?"

I'm now paranoid that this memo makes me seem pathetic. Then I think, *Maybe the memo is right.* "Thanks, yeah. Tough day."

I look out at the parking lot—large gray blocks of plowed snow piled in the corners, the line of buses sending up dark exhaust. My father went to this high school, and some of the teachers even re-member him. He wasn't okay in the head, either. He was the de-mented black sheep of the family, and I'm probably doomed to become like him, despite my mother's high hopes.

I sit down in a waiting-room chair and then I see my mother walk up to the front desk and sign in—she's got this down pat. She's wearing her scrubs decorated with cartoons of happy stick figures as if drawn by children. She works as an LPN in a pediatric ward, and she'll get docked for missing part of her shift. Her eyes, wet with worry, sweep the room and land on me. It's just the two of us, and sometimes I imagine us as two small glass figurines—the kind you'd find in a nativity scene near someone's Christmas tree—but we don't belong to anything.

She's the reason I didn't lean into the knife of the kid robbing me in the bathroom at group counseling. I couldn't do that to her. I can't abandon her, no matter how much I am a burden to her. We're just two glass figures and we could easily shatter.

Now that she's here, I want to kill Sprowitz for what he said about her in the cafeteria. I feel angry and guilty and ashamed all at the same time. I try to smile.

"There's nothing funny about any of this," she says, and then she walks over and sits next to me. "Tell me what happened." She doesn't wait for an answer. "What is with people? It's like"—she brushes my hair back from my face—"the world just wants us to hand our children over to it. You pour all this love in and then they just want to take it."

"I'm fine," I say. "I'm sorry."

She shakes her head. I know that I'm breaking her heart. She used to be lighter, happier. But since all of this mental stuff started happening to me, she seems almost haunted. She wanders the house late at night like she wants to ward something off. I wish I were the kind of girl who stood up straight and thrived in team sports and helped decorate proms.

"You can tell the principal you're sorry," my mother says. "Just nod and take responsibility. People respect that."

"But what if that's not the truth? Don't people respect honesty?"

"Not really. The truth isn't always simple. People like things simple."

The principal's door opens and Sprowitz walks out. He smiles at my mother, his lips all wet, his eyes narrowed. I want to grab his head and knee him in the face.

"Hey, Mrs. Maxwell," he says, low voiced.

"Move on, Brian," Principal Waybourne says, arms crossed. His jaw is tight.

Sprowitz waves. "Later, Mr. Waybourne."

When Principal Waybourne sees my mother, he uncrosses his arms, puts his hands in his pockets, and looks at the floor. "Ms. Maxwell," he says. "I'm glad you could make it."

Sometimes I forget the effect my mother has on men. My mother doesn't date. At all. She says she's not interested. But even in scrubs she's beautiful. She had me when she was only nineteen and my dad was twenty-one. Sometimes when she's not being so hard on herself, she says, "Your dad and I were kids. How could we have known what we were getting ourselves into?"

There's a lot I'll never know about my parents, but I like to imagine them like that—just kids who didn't know what they were getting themselves into. Honestly though, my father doesn't deserve forgiveness.

And here's Waybourne, now glancing at her in a way that makes me a little sick—as if Sprowitz weren't enough for today. "Hey, Principal Waybourne!" I say to get his eyes off her.

Waybourne's expression goes serious. "Hello, Alicia." He ushers us both into his office.

As we sit down in fake leather chairs, Principal Waybourne says to my mother, "Third time I've seen her this trimester."

"I know," my mother says. "We're trying to sort out the meds. Once we do, everything will settle. I promise. She's sorry. Aren't you? Tell him how sorry you are."

"I'm sorry," I say. "I'm sorry Brian Sprowitz punched my friend in the face."

Waybourne smiles, hangs his head low, and shakes it slowly. "See?" he says to my mother. "This isn't good."

"I'm doing the best I can."

"We're worried about you," Waybourne says. "That's all. We want to set a course. We want to get you going in the right direction."

"Let me show you our documentation," my mother says. She pulls out a piece of paper she's had for a year now and has already shown to Principal Waybourne plenty of times. It's so heavily creased that it's almost worn through. She spreads it on the desk. "Dr. Alex Maxwell. He's got Alicia going to Dr. Jane Larkin, and he's overseeing her treatment and prescriptions."

"The uncle, right?"

She nods. "He's Briggs-Wharton Chair in Neurobiology," she says. I've never understood what this means and I'm sure my mother doesn't either. "He's assured me that he can sort out Alicia's meds and that she has a really bright future." She pushes the letter toward the principal another few inches. "It's all in there."

"I know what it says," Principal Waybourne tells her. I know how Waybourne would describe me. "Troubled. Disturbed." In the old days, I'd probably be chained to the wall of an asylum already.

But Principal Waybourne sees the look on my mother's face after his last comment and retools. "Let's make the best of this. Let's do the right thing. I think I've found a workable solution."

"Oh, okay," my mother says. She picks up the letter and re-folds it.

"You know that this—disturbance—at lunch isn't the only issue. Alicia isn't prompt. She glazes over in class. She's failing Spanish, math, and economics."

I don't like it when they talk about me like I'm not there. I tap my sneakers.

My mother says, "Her math teacher hasn't ever really accepted any of Alicia's issues. She thinks it's all behavioral—"

"It's not just Mrs. Bartle. All of the teachers have serious concerns. Across the board."

"Sit up," my mother says to me, and I do, quickly, but I can't look at the two of them, so I look out the wide window—kids pouring out of the main door, herded through the metal detectors. I search for Hafeez, but don't see him. If he were brought in here, both his parents would show up. It makes a difference. Hafeez's parents are doing doctoral work in something physics related. My mother, a single mom, has a wrinkled doctor's note.

"And she has these, uh, medical conditions that make her un-reachable from time to time. This has an effect on the other kids. And this isn't the first altercation she's found herself in."

"I'm aware of that," my mother says, "but—"

Waybourne lifts a hand. "Let's talk to Alicia about this." He looks at me. "The thing you've got to figure out, Alicia," Waybourne says, "is that you've only got one life to live. Only one! It's precious. Do you want to throw it away? Your one life? Or do you want to do something with it?"

My mother looks at me as if she's desperate to hear my answer, as if she can't breathe until she knows if I'm going to do something with my life. *Only one!* I think, and I feel it in my chest, pressure so tight I could burst. I see the moment that kid pulled the knife, how surprised he was when I put my iPod down on the edge of the sink, raised my hands in the air, and whispered, "Just do it! Go ahead! Split me open." And I took a step toward her. What did she expect, robbing screwups at a counseling session?

I say, "Isn't that a soap opera? *One Life to Live?*"

My mother shakes her head and looks away. I can't help but feel like there's a darker answer to the question, and no one wants to hear it. Sometimes all I want to say to her is that breaking her heart kind of breaks mine.

Waybourne twists in his chair and says, very solemnly, "We've got a special track here, Ms. Maxwell. It's for kids who need more attention. Isn't that what Alicia needs? More attention?"

"The Freaks Track?" I say. Sprowitz is in Freaks. He'd make my life hell. I'd be a Future Bottomfeeder of America. The anxiety kicks in. "Is that what you mean?"

"She has a very high IQ!" my mother says loudly. She's wearing lipstick, I notice, maybe put on to sweeten Waybourne.

Waybourne blinks at her. He has very pale lashes. His scalp shines. "It's not special ed. It's just extra help. It's meant to—"

My mother puts her hands up. "Do you realize what that would mean? She won't stand a chance at colleges! She'll be . . ."—she's looking for the right word—". . . derailed!"

"Ms. Maxwell," Waybourne says quietly and calmly. "Don't you know?"

"Know what?"

"It doesn't matter how smart she is. She's already derailed herself."

My mother doesn't move. For a full ten seconds, she does nothing. There are voices on the other side of the office door. A bus engine revs. Then she stands up so fast her chair squawks against the floor. She says, "Let's go, Alicia."

I stand up, too. My mother walks to the door, opens it, and I walk out in front of her. She leans back in through the door frame and says, "You can't do this. We know our rights, you understand? You and I won't discuss this again. I'll have someone call you on our behalf."

My uncle. That's who she's going to send in. My father's brother—the doctor of brain science, the one who pays for my therapy sessions and all of my meds, the one who dug his way out of Southie by applying himself, the Maxwell who's not my father, the one who's better than we are, the one who can save us, the one we're *indebted* to.

The one I can't stand.

CHAPTER FOUR

MY MOTHER grips the wheel, her jaw tight. The warm air from the car heater is tinged with exhaust. I put my fists up to the vents then open my palms. My hands are shaking. I'm about to try to explain the flashes in the cafeteria. I want her to know that I'm not trying to cause these problems. But she pushes her phone at me as we pull up to a red light and tells me to call Alex. "Put it on speaker."

"Are you sure?" I find the number and press the green call button. "Wouldn't you rather talk behind my back?"

She doesn't smile. She never wants to ask Alex for help. In fact, she'd been completely cut off from my father's side of the family until I started having issues. She seemed to want a clean break, but she didn't know anyone else to turn to. Alex is a specialist and, I have to admit, he's totally and completely on our side. He *wants* to help. And he is this link to my father, even though he's nothing like my father, and that's probably a good thing. Still, my mother never wants to ask anyone for help, and she has to swallow a lot of pride on my behalf. He's all we've got.

The phone's ringing, and I'm hoping he doesn't pick up, but then he does. "Francesca?" He has caller ID so he knows who it is. "Everything okay?" He assumes something's wrong because my mother only calls when something is. I don't *hate* Uncle Alex. It's just, I'm like this problem he has to fix, and I will never be able to make it up to him. And I can't help but feel that obligation. That's what I hate. My uncle even tried to help my dad, but apparently the old man was a lost cause. I'm my uncle's next big failure.

"We've had an incident at school." Her eyes flick toward me and then away. "I was wondering if you could help."

"Anything," he says, and I imagine his thin face, his thick short hair tinged gray, his sport coat. In the summer, he kayaks, and he's offered to take me, but I can't bring myself to do it. Sometimes I wonder if I could let go of my father—really let go of even the idea of him racing through my hallucinations—I might be able to see Uncle Alex as a father figure. Would that be so bad? "Just tell me what you need," he says.

My mother fills Alex in a little, keeping it short. She knows how busy he is and hates to take up his time.

"Hey," Alex says to my mom on the phone, "we can help Alicia. She knows we can." I heard him telling my mother once that he feels guilty his brother is a screwup. My grandfather on that side of the family lost it, too. It's hereditary. And on the one hand I agree: my father did screw up, he left us. But on the other, I have this weird loyalty to him: he is still my father. "Listen, head over to Jane's office. I'll call ahead and ask her if she can clear her schedule, squeeze Alicia in."

"Thank you," my mother says. "Really, we can't tell you how much this means to us." Gratitude—that's the real payment here. I wish it were money, which is simpler.

"Don't worry about it. I'll call the principal tomorrow. I'll get him to back off. Maybe we can readjust the meds a little. Listen, tell Alicia I'll be at her party. I'll check in with her then."

I'd forgotten about my birthday party. I'm about to turn sixteen. My mother throws a party every year, which feels like a punishment for growing up. The Butlers come—the elderly couple two doors down with the dog whose hind leg was shattered by Sprowitz; Jill, my mom's friend from work; and Uncle Alex. Both sets of grandparents are gone; my mother's parents died when she was my age. She finished high school in foster care. I supposedly met my dad's parents when I was little. I only remember them from photos. We eat nachos and cake.

"Thanks for everything," my mother says.

Alex lowers his voice so it's soft, almost scratchy. "And I'll check on you. After all the things you do for other people, you need to be taken care of, too. You sometimes forget that." His voice is too intimate. Maybe I'm paranoid, but sometimes I think he's flirting with her in ways that he could always say were just him being nice.

"Hey!" I say, so Alex knows I've been there all along. "I'll see you at my party! Looking forward to it!"

There's an awkward pause. "Alicia, be straight with Jane," he says, like he's now my dad all of a sudden. "She's on your side."

"I know," I say. Jane means well. I kick at my backpack wedged between my sneakers on the floorboard.

After he hangs up, my mother and I drive in silence for a few minutes and then she starts in: "Uncle Alex isn't going to be able to clean up after you forever. One more slip and you'll have to go into that program. Next time I won't even call him."

I think of my father, telling me to get lost and stay lost. I'm useless—worse than useless. I'm a burden. I feel sick knowing it. I wonder if this is how my father started to spin out. Was he put on something like the Freaks Track? I stare out the window. "I have a question about Dad." I can't look at my mom. She hates questions about my father, and I hate seeing the way her face pinches, as if she's physically in pain.

"What is it?" she asks flatly.

"The restraining order." I've never asked about. I guess I didn't want to know.

"What about it?"

"Why'd you have to get one?"

She's silent for so long that I wonder if she's going to answer at all. Finally, she says, "We needed borderlines."

"You mean, boundaries, like emotional boundaries in a relationship?"

"No," she says. "I mean it the way I said it." And I know by her tone that the conversation is over.

We wind out of Southie, onto I-93, and eventually exit into Westwood, where the streets are clean and tree-lined. The yards are wide. People keep their shrubs tidy and salt their icy sidewalks in case an old person is out.

My mom pulls up to Jane's house. Her home office is crammed into what would probably be a small family room, but Jane has no husband, no kids. I like this about her. She's alone, so maybe she understands when I talk about feeling cut off.

"I'll be waiting here," my mother says. She reaches out and touches my jacket. "You have to just try to hang on. Just a little while longer." She looks at me searchingly and squeezes my arm, then lets go. She's scared in a way I haven't ever seen before.

"Why just a little longer? What do you mean?"

She shakes her head and puts both hands back on the wheel, staring straight ahead. "Alex doesn't want me to tell you; he's not sure it'll work."

"Tell me anyway." It's just the two of us; we have to rely on each other.

She sighs. "There's a surgery. It could free you of all of these issues, for good."

I feel a flash of panic in my chest. "Surgery?"

"This has been what Alex has been working on all these years. One of the things. He thinks it could be an overdeveloped part of the brain. Wait for him to talk with you about it, okay?"

"Okay." I'm not sure what to feel. Surgery that could make me normal, but also cut me off from those worlds, my father? It's all I have of him. Sad, I know, but I couldn't ever let go of him. I don't think I could ever explain this to my mother—or anyone. My father is unforgivable, but not when I see him in my hallucinations. He's different. We both are.

"If you can just really try for a little while longer, try to resist," she says softly.

And I wonder if she understands, in some way, how much I'd like to disappear into those hallucinations sometimes and just not come back. Could she know how I wanted to lean into the knife?

I nod, but I know I won't resist. I can't. She would never understand those other places, what it's like to suddenly be somewhere far away from everyone and everything in my own shitty little life.

"Be straight with Jane," she reminds me, "like Uncle Alex said."

"I will." I am never really straight with Jane, almost.

"Promise?"

"Promise."

CHAPTER FIVE

I WALK up to Jane's front door, dipping my head under some hanging planters with plants long since frozen and wilted over the sides. I swing my backpack over my shoulder, ring the bell, and wait. Eventually, I hear the familiar shuffling and turning of locks.

The door opens and there's Jane—small and narrow, rubbing her skinny arms. She waves to my mom and then tells me to come in. "It's freezing."

I step inside. She shuts the door, looks me over. "Are you okay?" Her voice is maternal in such a soft way that it catches me off guard, and then she gives me a hug. "Alex told me what happened. I'm sorry."

I almost tear up, maybe because I'm just exhausted, my defenses broken down. I wasn't expecting that kind of sudden tenderness. People ought to warn you before they do something like that. "I'm fine," I say.

She leads me down the hall to her office. I drop my backpack at the end of the slightly sagging love seat, sit down, and take in the small, familiar room. A fireplace that doesn't look like it ever gets used. An old oak desk against one wall. An armchair. A coffee table with an unlit candle. Built-in shelves packed with psych books, all of them describing one problem or another. The sheer number of things that can go wrong with someone actually makes me feel a little better. There's a painting of a sailboat tilting into the wind; it reminds me of the cruise ship and the speedboat.

Jane takes a seat in the armchair across from me.

I lean back. I still feel shaky. I remember my biology teacher talking about the aftereffects of hypothermia, the uncontrollable trembling. That's how I feel now. "Do you know anything about geography?" I ask.

"A little," she says. "Why?"

"Do you know a river called the Dnieper?"

She stands up and walks to a row of old encyclopedias. She pulls out one of the books, flips through it. "Dnieper? Here we go. It's a major European river that flows through Russia, Belarus, and Ukraine, eventually flowing into the Black Sea." She looks up. "Why do you ask? Something school related?"

"No." It's real, but I've never heard of it. "Just curious."

She looks at me for a moment. "Okay, let's start over." She slips the book back into its slot and sits down again. "The hallucination. What sparked it?"

"Well, there were two rounds of it just this morning, which means they're getting worse, right?"

"Let's try not the judge the hallucinations. Let's just examine them."

"Well, one happened during a multiple-choice test, and the other was when I was at lunch." I don't want to get into what Sprowitz said about my mom. Sometimes I just can't break it to adults that kids can be so sick in the head.

"You can opt out of multiple choice," Jane says.

"I know. I'd like to stop picking at my cuticles, too. I don't even know I'm doing it really until it starts bleeding. Should I tape my fingertips or something?"

"We can work on some more relaxation techniques," she says.

I suck at relaxation techniques; they make me more worked up than before. I look at the boat in the painting then back at Jane. A button is missing on her sweater. "This kid got pissed off and hit my friend Hafeez. Then I started flashing."

"And how were these hallucinations different?"

I lean forward, elbows on my knees. "Do you think you can know something in a hallucination that you don't know in real life?"

"Like what?"

"Just like a fact or even part of some foreign language. Not to be fluent or anything, but just to understand some."

"I think in a dream your brain can make you believe you're speaking a different language when, if fully awake, you'd really be speaking gibberish. As for facts, I don't know. Maybe you could know a fact without remembering you know it."

"I guess."

"What did you see in the hallucination?"

"I was with my father." I picture him now in the back of the speedboat. He looked so tired but still rugged, his dark windblown hair and straight jaw. He was fit, muscular and strong, his tattoo like a vine curling up from his wrists. "I talked to him. We were on a cruise ship at first, and it was sinking. Later, he talked back to me. But like he knew I was there. Me. That's never happened before."

I get up and walk around the sofa, doing one little lap. "It felt real. I was there, and then he told me to go back, and everything started to shake, and then—I was back." I can't say to her what he really said earlier: *Get lost and stay lost.*

The heater kicks on. I hear the soft exhale from the register.

"Back?" She seems to be concentrating really hard on what I'm saying, like she's adding something up in her head. I hope so. I'm tired of the old answers—this med or that. Could there really be a way out of this for me, even if I have to get my head cut open?

"I was in the cafeteria. With Hafeez and the fight. And he had a bloody lip."

"What did you feel—in your body—when this was happening?"

"I don't know. It hurt."

"How? Where?"

All those quick pains shooting all over me and that feeling like my chest was going to rip open. I don't want to sound like I'm trying to make it bigger than it is. Though it felt so big I'm not sure I can really describe it in a way that makes sense. I shrug. "I don't know."

Jane's fingers are all laced up, and her eyes are locked on the far wall—all those books. I've never seen her look like this. I don't like the silence. I don't know how to read her expression. "What's wrong?" I ask.

"Nothing," she says. "It's just interesting."

"You know what's interesting? The principal wants to send me to the Freaks Track."

"What's that?"

"A special track for screwed-up kids. Like me. My mom seems to think Alex can talk him out of it."

"I'm sure he can. That's not an appropriate place for you to be. We've always wanted to keep you mainstreamed."

"Staying mainstreamed, that's a goal? I'm insulted," I say, pretending to be disgusted.

"I'm sorry. I didn't mean to—"

"No, it's fine. I should aspire to mainstream. I should be so lucky." I'm pissed all of a sudden.

Jane shifts in her chair. I know she doesn't like it when I get angry, but she wouldn't ever call me on it. I'm supposed to feel comfortable with my emotions in here, even anger. She says, "Tell me more."

"In one of the flashes, I saw a boy. I was in this really nice house but it was completely falling apart. Actually that whole place seemed like it was—I don't know—cracking." I remember his lips so clearly, the way he was talking to me, but I could no longer hear him.

"What did he look like?" Jane scoots forward in her seat. Something about the boy—or the destruction?—has caught her attention. I wonder if these are signs I'm really crazy.

I shrug. I want to tell her that he was kind of beautiful, but that sounds embarrassing. "He had black hair and these wild eyes— really, really light blue."

"How old was he?"

This seems like an odd question: why would his age matter? "About the same as me, I guess," I say. But then again, he was so thin, and haunted looking, he could be older. I don't feel like talking about him anymore. He's just made up, like my father in the speedboat. Do I really just want a father that badly? It'd be a better fantasy if the places weren't filled with billowing smoke, drones, and gun-wielding thugs. Anyway, the places aren't real. The boy isn't, either. I have to remember that. I'm just a screwed-up kid who aspires to be mainstream. "He's fake anyway, right? A figment of my imagination."

"The imagination is powerful, Alicia. It can hold a lot of information that can help us understand who we are."

"What if I don't want to understand who I am? If you were me, would you?"

"Yes."

I shrug. I want to say *Bully for you*—it's an expression that Mr. Butler, my neighbor, uses. He and his wife will probably bring their dog, Artie, his amputation still fresh, with them to the party.

"You said things in that one hallucination were falling apart.

How?" Jane's pushing me. Her voice is as hard-edged as I've ever heard it.

I take a breath and just hold it. How could I possibly explain that world? Decaying, beautiful, broken, dying . . . I want to go back. I want to feel it again. I shrug.

"Alicia, if you want to improve—"

"I just can't explain it. It's not possible."

She stands and walks to the front of her oak desk. She opens the top drawer. She lifts something small—a square piece of paper, a photograph? I can't see, but whatever it is, she's struck by it. Her face softens.

Then, quickly and nervously, she reaches for something on the back of her desk, blocked by a stack of books. I hear the click of some kind of button pressed, something being turned on or off. Has she been recording this?

She doesn't look at me; instead she says, "Tell me more about the boy in that world. Tell me as much as you can." Her voice is quiet, urgent.

"Why?"

"It's important, Alicia." She's very serious, suddenly intense or maybe just scared. "Anything else about this place? Or him? Anything?"

"What's it matter? None of it's real. I mean, it's just my weird brain, riffing, right?"

She takes a deep breath. "Right. Look, Alicia, you're going to be fine. Trust me. You'll get through this."

"Of course I'll be fine. I aspire to mainstream. It's all about setting really shitty goals for yourself."

Jane lets that slide. She reaches back into the drawer, hits the button again. I hear another click. "Your uncle wants to discuss upping your anti-anxiety meds. Is that something you think would help?"

Aren't *they* supposed to tell me what'll help? I'd ask her about the surgery, but I'm not supposed to know anything about it. I sit down on the couch heavily and lean over, holding my head in my hands. My head feels swimmy. My heart's beating too fast. "I'm tired."

"You've had a hard day."

This isn't something I can sleep off. It's the fatigue of carrying around this feeling of near-implosion. I never told her what I said to the kid who robbed me at knifepoint. I never told anyone. I know what happens to kids who confess wanting to lean into a knife.

"I don't feel good. I might throw up." It's true. The room is lurching like that ship. I feel like I could lose it all over the fancy rug.

"Do you want to use the bathroom?"

"No, I want to go." I stand up, feeling dizzier, and move quickly to the door.

"Let me walk you out."

"Don't. My mom's waiting."

Jane nods, rubbing her arms again.

I leave her there, walk down the hall, running one hand along the wall to keep myself steady. I get to the front door and step outside. I see the back of my mom's car, idling to keep the heat on. I stand there a minute trying to take the deep cleansing breaths that Jane's taught me. They don't help.

I take a few steps down the front walk but then realize I don't have my backpack.

I rush back to the house, not bothering with the bell, and walk down the hall. Jane isn't in her office.

I feel hot, in my core. I've broken a sweat. I see my backpack, grab it, swing it over my shoulder, and head back down the hall.

But then I hear her voice, coming from another room off the hall. The door is slightly open. I hear my name. I tiptoe up the hall and pause near the door, knowing I should keep going.

"She broke through," Jane says. Then silence; she's listening.

"This is definitely it. She told me she spoke to Ellington and that he talked back. He knew it was her."

Ellington is my father's name. I freeze, straining to hear, as if I could pick up on who's at the other end of the call.

Jane's listening again, like she's taking instructions. "Yes, yes. Okay . . . But Olsson, he'll come for her now that she's broken through. He'll risk everything. I'm sure you know that."

Now that I broke through? She can't mean my father; he wouldn't come for me. It's been too long. And who's Olsson?

She hangs up, and I walk quickly back down the hall. I step outside, shutting the door quietly behind me, and run down the path, still dizzy. I slam down the latch on the gate of her picket fence, skinning a knuckle, then push off a post. I slide into the passenger's seat, and shut the door. "Let's go."

"What's wrong?" My mother looks like she's ready to go inside and talk to Jane herself.

"Nothing. Let's just go."

"Something's wrong. What is it?"

"I don't know what you're talking about."

"You're out of breath."

"Am I?"

"And you're early."

"I ran out of things to say."

"It's a two-way street, Alicia. If you want to feel better, you have to be willing to work for it." She puts the car in gear and starts driving.

"I will. I got tired." I look out the window.

We pass a car parked on a side street. The driver looks up from a cell phone and seems surprised to see me. After we pass by, the car pulls out. Is he following us?

I reach into my pocket and grab my pill bottle. My finger is smeared with blood from the spot where I skinned my knuckle on the gate. I blot it on the knee of my jeans and slide a pill into my palm where all the lines converge. I pop the pill and lean back, closing my eyes.

The boy's face is there, his blue eyes, his lips and bright teeth. Beautiful. I'm glad I didn't tell Jane. He's *my* hallucination, after all.

As the pill starts to take the world down a notch, I hear my mother whisper something so softly I can barely make it out. "Don't leave me. Don't disappear on me."

"I won't," I say. "I promise."

"What?" she asks. "What was that?"

"I'm going to shut my eyes." I don't want her to know that I'm fading out. I don't close my eyes. I stare out the window.

"You should rest," she says.

The windshield blurs and disappears. My breath is shallow. Light pours out of everything around me, including my outstretched hands.

The blood on my knuckle is already drying up. And the pain comes, but it's not all over my body. It's all fixed in one spot—my bicep. *Go on. Take me. Take me somewhere.* I grab the muscles in my arm and push. The pain gets sharper. . . .

. . . I'm lying on my stomach on a bed in what looks like an old hotel room that used to be nice—the faded, dusty red-velvet drapes drawn. My shoulder burns with pain. And I know that I'm back in the world where I got shot on the cruise ship, where I talked to my dad and he knew it was me. But he isn't here.

I see myself in a huge tarnished mirror. An old man is leaning over my back, stitching me up—the bullet wound. He has a long drooping mustache and wears a dark suit. He digs into my shoulder with the needle, and I feel a roar of pain.

Where is my father? Why isn't he here? I'm alone, and this is what scares me the most. Who are these people?

A woman is yelling in the bathroom. I understand only bits and pieces of her Russian—maybe she speaks a dialect—*"She's lucky he got her out."* She walks into the room and points to a big bulky television, airing footage of a mushroom cloud like the atomic bomb. She has bloody towels bundled in her arms. She's saying, *"The birds will fall from the sky, like Chernobyl, like Japan."*

Each time the old man digs the needle in, my head feels like it's going to explode from the pain. My vision blurs.

I turn my head from the television and the woman with the bloody sheets; I know it's my blood that's soaked the towels. I can feel the old man's needle suturing the wound in my back.

Lying beside me on the bed is a tin tray holding a single bullet, glazed in a thin smear of blood. My blood. My hand starts ringing with pain. My vision dims and dims like someone slowly turning down the lights.

And then I can't see anything at all. . . .

. . . I'm back in the car, and my mother says, "Hey, you awake? We're home."

My house.

Its scuffed front door with the chipped brown paint.

Its small pitted yard.

The cold.

CHAPTER SIX

SIX DAYS later, it's my fifteenth birthday. From my bedroom upstairs, I hear the regulars my mother has invited to the party starting to arrive. I know it's time to go downstairs, but I hate these parties. I have to pretend I don't. They give my mother some comfort—that I am still a little kid she throws parties for, that things are okay, that nothing has to change.

I've spent the last six days trying not to think of the beautiful boy from my hallucinations. He's not real, I keep telling myself, but still he keeps popping into my mind during homework and classes and bus rides and when I try to fall asleep at night. I haven't had any more extended hallucinations since the day of the cafeteria brawl, but the flashing comes more often and every decision feels like it's tearing me apart, literally.

My window is iced at the edges even though the heat's turned up for the guests, the baseboards ticking. I look out the window and see the row of muddy yards across the street. One still has a plastic reindeer. It's been kicked to its side.

A stray dog, ribs like bony spikes, skitters down the street. I watch it pass Sprowitz's house. I usually avoid looking at his place—a depressing brown house, its chain-link fence curling in on itself, its windows pink from the insulation lining that's probably not good to breathe, the crumbling driveway. The house has this dead stare, and I wonder what it's like for him to live there with strangers. Didn't he have a home once? Family? I don't know whether it would be better to have had family and lost them or never to have had them at all. I hate Sprowitz, but I feel for him, too.

And then I notice that one of the upper bedroom windows isn't fully covered. There's a pale hole where the insulation has been pulled aside.

It's not a pale hole at all—it's a face.

It's Sprowitz.

Is he looking at me looking at him? Is he waiting for a glimpse of my mother?

I flip him the bird. I know that he'll make me pay for it. He's avoided me at school this past week, or I've successfully avoided him—hard to say.

I expect him to give me the finger back but he doesn't.

His face disappears. The pink insulation fills the void.

Hafeez has texted a bunch of times: *You sure you don't want me to come over?*

Me: *Trust me. It's not going to be any fun. I'll save you a piece of cake.*

Hafeez: *Birthdays are overhyped bullshit. They've been no fun since we stopped beating up piñatas. If candy can't rain down on your head, why have a party at all?*

I close my eyes and think of being a kid. Most people my age can't wait to get older, to get out. But I would gladly go back to when none of this crazy shit was happening to me.

I've started to doubt everything. Did I really overhear the conversation that Jane had on the phone, or am I just going insane—like freaking out about people following me in traffic? My paranoia is almost constant no matter how many pills I take.

I've been thinking and rethinking my hallucinations—what sets me off and which images appear. I've made charts of each of the repeating hallucinations—what I look like in them, what my father's like, if I see him at all, and how each place seems to be deteriorating. I've come up with shorthand names for them in my notebook.

Cruise ship—where I got shot with my father as the ship sank.
Bulldog—where I met the old man.
Where the boy is—where I live in a mansion that overlooks a wasteland.

I've written tons of facts about the Dnieper River, the Volga, drones, contaminated water, and A-bomb mushroom clouds.

I flip through my notes, pages and pages of them, my doodles of trees in all of the margins.

Worthless. All of it.

Nothing is getting me any closer to some clear understanding of what I've been seeing or why. I hate how nothing makes sense. I hate my birthday. I hate the shitty reindeer in the neighbor's yard. I hate Sprowitz eyeing us from across the street.

I want to punch the window—one pane at a time, just drive my bare fist through the glass until my knuckles are a bloody mess.

I stare down at my notebook and see the word "blood" staring back at me. It's the part where I explain how I skinned my knuckle on Jane's gate.

I turn back a few pages to the fight with Sprowitz. And I see "bloody lip."

I flip back another page and read about the little piece of paper I tore from my Spanish test—the "blood" from my cuticle.

All this week, I've just been flashing between hallucinations, never landing. But if there's a cut, a scrape, a bloody lip . . .

My mother calls from downstairs, "Alicia, you coming? Everyone's here!"

"Coming!" I walk to my bedroom door, but just before I reach for the knob, I hesitate, and in this small momentary indecision—should I go now or wait a little longer?—my heartbeat picks up. I feel like a knife's been plunged into my collarbone, and then there's the ripping feeling in my sternum. Jesus.

My knees buckle. I drop to the floor. My breathing is jagged. I manage to call out, "Just a minute!"

I think again, *What if there's blood?*

I lurch to my desk and pull open a junk drawer. I rummage quickly, the pain stabbing my collarbone and my chest, and I pull out an old compass I haven't used since middle-school geometry, but the point is sharp enough to draw blood.

My hands shaking, I poke the meat of my palm, a sharp sting. A bead of blood rises—quick and dark red.

I push on the ache in my collarbone, but still, it's like I can't pinpoint it, can't really get at it. I roll to my back.

Okay, I say to myself, urging some inner engine. *C'mon.*

I stare at the blood.

And I feel the floor start to give beneath me.

I look at the ceiling; the dark water stain overhead shifts and swirls. *It's my birthday. I'm sixteen . . . And I don't know what the hell I'm turning into.*

The room seems to shatter, its pieces scattering. . . .

. . . The wind is hot and dry in my face.

An abandoned development with scorched bare yards.

A distant field with one sickly cow, stalled oil pumps, frozen against the horizon.

"This way." It's him. The boy with the blue eyes. His face isn't streaked with dirt like the last time I saw him. But his hair is a little shaggy and wild, and he hasn't shaved in a while. I'm stunned to find myself with him again. I'm following him across a field that's pocked with holes. I know what I look like here with my bleach-blond hair. I try to smooth my hair down and I wish I looked like myself, me. Even though I'm not known for having any fashion sense and maybe sometimes wear too much eyeliner, I suddenly wish he just knew me, the real me.

Up ahead is a chain-link fence, tall and topped with razor wire, around a trailer park. A large placard, QUARANTINE written on it.

He stops in front of a tree that's half in bloom, half dead, as if split down the middle. One side is puffed with petals, and the other looks like a claw. "This is what I wanted to show you."

I touch the bark, its thin, papery casing. I remember a Plath poem about a forest that turns to ash. I whisper, "Ash," trying to remember the rest.

"What's that?"

"Nothing," I say, not wanting to sound like a poser, I quickly add, "Why is it half dead?"

"The question is why is it half alive," he says. His lashes are so dark they look wet.

I walk around the tree, looking at its limbs, the small rows of buds and then the dead limbs, brittle and dark.

"How's the special treatment up there?" he asks, nodding to the rows of once-fancy houses I followed him from.

"My mother's sick," I say.

"My mother's dead," he says flatly. "We're the only ones now. It's just us."

"I didn't grow up in that house," I tell him. "That's not me. I've never had money like that."

His eyes widen. "Oh, hi. I get it. How long have you been here as, you know, *you*?"

"How do you know . . . ?" I'm stunned. It's like the moment when my father realized it was really me. "What do you mean, *me*?"

"Look, I'm glad it's you." He runs his fingers down a branch. "This tree is no accident. We only look at the blooming half," he tells me. "Before my mother died, she explained everything. Perception breeds reality, not the other way around."

"What are you talking about?"

He pulls a clump of tall dry weeds from the ground and shakes them.

The seeds break loose, drift, and then disappear, as if they never existed. "This world isn't being held in place anymore."

I lift my hand. "Can I try it?"

He nods. He hands the bouquet of stalks to me, my hand brushing his.

I touch a few seeds, feel their silky texture on my fingertips for only a second, and then they float off and disappear. "Why?" I whisper. "How?"

"Your dad needs to be looking into this. Tell him that Jax said we need him or this is all going to go away."

"Jax. That's your name."

"Yeah."

I want to say it over and over again. It feels like something has unlocked inside of me. "What's going to go away if my dad doesn't look into this?" I ask. Is my father here somewhere? Is he like an actor waiting just offstage? A ghost?

"The whole thing," Jax says.

This world? This place that feels embedded in me somehow?

Maybe I love it here because it isn't something I could ever really dream up. I don't have this good of an imagination, and because it's so wild, it feels more real.

"Wait," I say, because everything's growing paler and paler. Something is about to unwind in me—something that can't be put back together.

I can't feel my father's presence here. And some part of me is gone, too. I feel dizzy again, staggering. My hand starts to buzz with pain, and I want to tell it to shut up. I'm not ready to go.

Jax looks at me. "What is it?"

I want to ask him if he's real, if this world exists, but then wind picks up and a flock of birds kick up from a distant field and it's like their wings take pieces of the dirt, the sky, everything with them until there's nothing except chaos. . . .

CHAPTER SEVEN

BREATHLESS. I'M sitting on the edge of my bed, stunned that the blood theory worked. It's weirdly thrilling. I remember the feel of the seeds against my fingers and Jax's hand brushing mine. They've a stain of some kind, like the most real things I've ever felt. I go to the bathroom and wash the blood off my hand in the rusty sink, but I still feel his touch. I'm dizzy, shaking.

I walk downstairs to the kitchen where my mother isn't icing the cake so much as smothering it. But maybe that's my imagination. Ever since the talk with the principal, she's kept a close eye on me. Maybe I'm the one feeling smothered. "What took you so long?"

"Sorry. Got distracted. What can I do to help?" I feel like there's still static in my ears.

My mother turns and smiles at me, the smile she gives to her patients. She nods to a plastic bowl of chips and a tub of onion dip. "Bring that out to the guests. Say hello. Be respectful."

I grab the chips and dip and walk into the living room. People are talking about the fallout from the Red Sox, but as soon as they see me, everyone stops. Mr. and Mrs. Butler, who give me a card every year with a five-dollar bill folded inside, are sitting on the love seat, holding Arnie, whose amputation wound is wrapped in gauze. I think of Sprowitz, bashing the dog's leg. It makes me sick.

Uncle Alex is here, as promised, sitting in the only armchair. He's wicked fit, tall and broad. His polo shirt looks tailored, and his stiff gray hair is too expensive-looking to be a barber cut. He always smells expensive, too, wearing some cologne bought on another continent.

"Alicia," he says. "Happy birthday! Hope it's okay that I brought two of my research assistants. They've worked with me a long time." He points to two guys sitting on foldout metal chairs my mother hauled in from the shed. They don't seem to want to be here any more than anyone else, glancing out the windows, fidgeting in the chairs—and who could blame them? I don't want to be here. One of them, with the darker hair, looks familiar to me, but I can't say how.

"Fine by me."

The doorbell rings. Jane comes in, letting in a cold blast of air. "Happy birthday!" She's overly chipper.

"Hi," I say. I'm surprised to see her. It's like she's not really supposed to exist outside of her office. I wonder if she's being paid to observe me in my natural habitat.

"So glad to be here!" But she isn't glad to be here at all. Her eyes are skittish. She smiles at Alex and the others quickly, but she seems like she just wants to escape.

We all gather around the onion dip, awkward as hell.

Mrs. Butler tells me how pretty I've gotten. Mr. Butler updates me on Arnie. "Three more weeks before he's all healed up! They say bites are the worst because they tear the muscles and tendons."

"Bites?"

Mr. Butler nods, dips a nacho. "Yes, some other dog must've gotten to him."

"I thought—I thought you said his leg had gotten crushed somehow."

Mr. Butler frowns and shakes his head. "No. He was just too torn up to save the leg."

So did Sprowitz do something to Arnie or not? I can't think about it, because Mr. Butler wants to know when I'm going to get my driver's license. "Maybe soon," I say, but the truth is I can't shoot for it unless I can figure out how to get my grades up. And what if I flash while I'm driving? Jane asks if I made the onion dip. It's brutal how little there is to talk about.

Uncle Alex brings up college, which he's offered to pay for. "In a couple years, high school will be in your rearview mirror. You'll make us all proud." Even though I know Alex means well, it just reminds me that my own father isn't here saying it.

After a few more minutes of chatter, I decide to give them a break. "I've got to make a call."

"Oh," my mother says, walking into the room. "Are you expecting some friends?" It's her greatest hope, that a group of guys in khakis and button-downs will show up with a few girls wearing braces, and we'll complain about SAT prep, maybe even sing a song about it, in harmony—the things her own childhood was lacking.

"Yeah, maybe," I say. This will get me out of the house, since the reception on my crappy phone is best in the backyard. "Hafeez had this thing, but it might end early." Honestly, it'd be cruel to subject him to this depressing glimpse into my home life.

"We've got plenty to eat," she says.

I grab my jacket, walk out the sliding door, which doesn't really slide anymore; it's more of a jerking door. I pretend to make a call, in case my mother is watching from the kitchen window, and when I glance over my shoulder, she is.

I walk across the small deck into the yard, cordoned off by a sagging chain-link fence. I hold the phone to my ear and pace. It's cold and damp. The sky is a bruised gray.

Even though the hallucinations can scare the hell out of me, I wish I could have one now. I'd like to be somewhere, *anywhere* else, but especially in Jax's world. It feels so good to know his name, like I have a piece of him that won't go away.

I glance back to the house. My mother's no longer watching, so I shut the phone on my fake call, shove my hands in my jacket pockets, and sigh.

And then I hear my name, a man's voice, calling to me in a hoarse whisper.

"Alicia."

It's coming from behind the rusted-out shed in the back corner of our small lot.

I walk toward the shed slowly. It's not Hafeez but still I say, "Hafeez?" because that would make sense in a way.

No answer.

I walk all the way back to the part of the yard blocked by the metal shed. I turn the corner. "Hello?"

And there, tall and thick shouldered, a little roughed up and wrung out, is my father.

Ellington Maxwell. In the flesh.

I take a step back, instinctively. I'm too stunned to think of what to say. I don't even feel anything at first. I just take him in: thick head of dark hair, graying sideburns, stubbled jaw, faded jeans. Wool jacket, pilled at the elbows.

For a second, I have the impulse to shout for my mother. When I was a little kid, she taught me to shout for help if approached by a stranger—and, well, my dad is a stranger. I feel like my father has broken not just the restraining order but also some unspoken trust by showing up. One thing I could rely on him for was his absence, and now he's even messed that up.

But I'm not a kid anymore. And this is my father—a man I haven't seen since I was three years old, but then again, I just saw him a week ago—on the ship and on the speedboat.

I finally feel something like love, but it's so twisted up inside of me that it could be fear.

My father and I stare at each other.

Then he glances back toward the house.

My heartbeat speeds up. I have to say something. I have to use this time to get answers out of him, but what are my questions? I start to panic. Here is this man who dominates my mind, even though he's been completely absent—someone I want to know but am terrified to become.

My father looks bent, exhausted, but happy to see me. He might even be a little nervous himself.

"You're here." It's the only thing I can think of.

"You look beautiful. You've grown up." His shoes, leather ones that aren't warm enough for the weather, are cracked at the toes.

"You're not supposed to be here," I say, thinking of my mother telling me the reason why she got the restraining order. They needed *borderlines*. I still don't know why.

"I know I shouldn't be here," he says.

This isn't going well. Now that love and fear feel like anguish. I'm finally meeting my father again and we're going to fail at this. We don't know how to be father and daughter. "Maybe you should leave," I say, not wanting him to go. "It's a party."

I look at the neighbor's caved-in aboveground pool, our shed—mottled with rust. I imagine my mother walking to the shed to get the metal folding chairs and then walking back to the house. Was my father here then? Watching?

"I know it's your birthday. I want you to have this." He holds out a present—a small thing wrapped messily in comic-strip newspaper.

"I don't want anything from you." But I know what I've said isn't true. "Not anymore." This feels a little more honest, but not much. When I was little, I wanted him around so badly that I seemed to carry that wanting with me everywhere. I tried to stop as I got older, knowing it was useless. He's here. He wants to give me a gift. I can't make it easy for him.

I stare at the ground—my mom's trowel wedged in the frozen dirt—then I make myself turn, start to walk back to the house. It's a test. Will he follow me into the middle of the backyard or will he stay hidden, like a coward? What's he willing to risk?

When I turn back, I see he has followed me, standing where anyone could see him, the present tucked under one arm.

"Alicia," he says. "You ever get a feeling that there's another version of yourself? A better version, maybe?"

Is this his attempt at an apology? "Shut up." I say it without even thinking. I've been angry at him for a long time.

"I wish I was a better person," my father says. "I keep one version of myself hidden away—the good one who's tried to do the right thing."

"I wish I knew that version of you."

"You know me better than you think." He offers the present again. "Take it and just promise me you won't toss it."

I walk up to my father like I'm going to take the gift, but I don't. "You left us. You abandoned us. Can't you pretend to regret it?" It's like all I want to do is hug him but I can't cut through all the sadness and anger.

"I have infinite regrets. I love you. And . . ." He looks up at the house, and I look, too. No one's at the windows. "I remember the first time I saw your mother. I knew I was looking at the face of the girl who'd break my heart in a million ways—still, it was worth it." He offers the gift again. "Here."

This time, I take it. I look at the newsprint. *Ziggy. The Far Side.* Do they still run these cartoons? It's oddly shaped and small enough to fit into one of my jacket pockets.

"They're going to be out here any minute," he says. "Listen to me. Something's going to happen to you. When it does, you'll know it."

I try to laugh this off. "A lot of things have happened to me," I tell him. "What are you even talking about?"

"When this thing happens, you'll have some real power, Alicia. You need to get off the meds, stop trying to mask the truth of who you are."

How does my father know about the pills? "I think you've given up the right to give fatherly advice, don't you?"

"You're right." My father rubs his jaw, the edge of a tattoo peeking out from under his shirt sleeve. And there's more of it— branchlike tendrils wrapping around his wrist and neck. And those scars on his left hand, lots of nicks. He tries again. "This isn't going to make too much sense now, but that world, where you saw the boy—it's real. Jax is real."

I take a quick breath that's so cold my lungs burn. I only told Jane about him. Did my father talk to Jane somehow? But, no. I didn't know his name when I talked to her about him. "How do you know about Jax?" I manage to ask. I'm shivering, more from nerves than the cold.

He doesn't answer. He's urgent now, his face taut with emotion. He glances at the windows again. "Tell Jax's mother that if her world starts to die, I mean *really* die, she has to get the atlas out. I probably won't be able to help."

"I can't tell her anything."

"Why not?"

"She's dead," I say.

"Jesus." My father's eyes fill with tears. He stares at the sky, then locks eyes back on me. "There's no one to get him out. If that world dies, he'll die with it and the atlas will be lost."

"I've got to go." I assume he's high though he doesn't really look it.

"Don't tell anyone Jax exists, Alicia."

"Well, he doesn't!" I tell him. "They're not real people! They can't be!"

"You're wrong," my father says, shaking his head like he's fighting for patience. "You're not crazy. And you have to get away from here, from Alex. You can't trust him. He thinks I stole something from him, but I never did. And Jax has a powerful gift. You might have one, too—a different one. But you're both too green, too young." He's muttering to himself for that last part more than talking to me. He seems shaky, nervous.

"Look, Jax is going to need your help and you might need his. Promise me you'll try to get him out of that world. And the atlas . . ." His voice trails off and his expression tightens like he's trying to do a complex calculation in his head. He's clearly worried about Jax and this atlas, and the possibility of losing both.

Maybe my dad's a madman, but what really scares me is that little bits of what he's saying make sense to me—and probably only me. "You're crazy, right? I don't believe anything you're saying." I'm trying to sound like I'm accusing him, but my voice has gone soft. "Everyone's always told me that you're not right in the head."

I can feel the panic spreading in my chest. But the thing is I want to believe that there's some better version of myself, like he said. I want to be that person, and it feels like life or death—an ending or a beginning.

My father puts his hands on my shoulders, and this time he's smiling a little, mostly in his eyes. He's trying to be reassuring. "Just please trust me. After this thing happens, you're going to find out I'm not such a stranger after all."

"*What's* going to happen?"

My father opens his mouth to say something, but just then the sliding door bumps open. My mother calls my name. By the time I turn, she's already seen my father. She looks stricken. She grips the railing of the deck. Her breath fogs the air around her.

"Francesca," my father says.

"You." Her voice is barely above a whisper, but it carries in the cold air. I expect her to be angry, afraid, but I see something else, too.

My father takes a step toward her; she shakes her head once, and he stops. I feel dizzy from the sight of them together, the way they're looking at each other.

"This is the end of me, Francesca," my father says. "I'm the only one still free."

"Then why are you here?"

"I came back because she needs me. Can't you see that?"

"She needs a chance at a normal life. Can't *you* see *that?*"

My father looks at the ground. My mother covers her mouth. She looks like she's about to cry. And then I get it in the way she tilts her head: she still loves my father. Alex calls her from inside the house.

"Go," she says to Ellington. "Now. Hurry!"

My father grabs my arm. "I never took anything from Alex that belonged to him," he says quickly. He turns to go, but it's too late.

Alex steps outside, sees my father, asks my mother if she's okay. "Did he hurt you?"

"You know I'd never do that," my father says.

Alex glances at him and back at my mother.

She shakes her head, the wind whipping her hair. "I'm fine."

Jane comes out, too, hugging herself in the cold. Her eyes land on Ellington and her face stiffens with surprise. I think of what I overheard her saying: *He'll come for her. . . . He'll risk everything.* She was talking about my father.

Alex's research assistants lumber out onto the deck. "What's going on?" one of them asks.

My father grabs me and hugs me. He whispers, "You've been in those other worlds. They're real. You can move between them. You're a spandrel, Alicia. A spandrel." And then he pulls back and takes in my face. "*I am, I am, I am.* You are, you are, you are. Make your own map."

I'm breathless. A spandrel? What does that even mean? And he's quoting part of a Plath poem, one of my favorites. How does he know how much I love those words?

And in this moment I know that he's telling the truth. There's something going on that I don't understand; there's something bigger here. In this moment, I trust him. That's all I know.

Then my father releases me and walks backward, his arms open wide. "Hey, I was just going," my father shouts to Alex. "No need to get physical."

"You shouldn't be here," Alex says. "You know the rules."

"Screw you and your rules!" my father shouts, and he looks flushed with sudden anger.

Alex calls to his assistants, "Get him out of here," and, just like that, they charge down the steps.

My father says, "You think I'm going to run? I'm right here."

There's something brave and stupid and strong about my father, something that I can't help but admire.

And then, as if it comes from some old instinct, my mother shouts, "Run, Ellington!"

My father looks at her, his expression sad and heartbroken. He doesn't run. He doesn't even brace himself.

The assistants are young and fast, and within seconds one of them tackles Ellington to the ground, twisting an arm behind his back and shoving his face into the ice-crusted ground.

"Lay off!" I shout, running over to them. "Stop! Leave him alone!"

Alex walks toward me and blocks my view of my father, as if protecting me from something I shouldn't see, but my father takes it as a threat.

"You've got me now," my father says. "You'll leave her alone then, okay. That's my daughter!" I've never heard my father claim me, and I never thought I would. His ruddy cheeks are streaked with dirt. As the two assistants haul him to his feet, one of them sneers a smile at me—the one I thought I recognized earlier. And right then I know exactly where I saw him before: he was driving the car that pulled out behind my mother when we were leaving Jane's office. Alex has these guys tailing me? One of the assistants jerks my father hard, and my father jerks back to right himself.

"Stop them!" I shout at Alex.

Alex opens his arms wide, looking exhausted, like this is one long battle—and maybe it has been. He looks like he just wants this whole thing to be over. "I'm doing everything I can to help you, Alicia. To protect your mother and you. Do you hear me?"

It all sounds condescending to me. He's just treating me like a child. I want to yell at him, but my mother would kill me if I so much as talked back to him.

Still, I'm about to go off just as Mr. and Mrs. Butler walk onto the deck, Arnie's yapping in Mr. Butler's arms.

"What's happened?" Mrs. Butler asks.

"What in the goddamn?" Mr. Butler says.

"Yes!" I say. "What in the goddamn?"

"Let's go back inside," Jane says, herding them through the sliding door.

"Take him to the car," Alex tells his assistants, who pull Ellington across the yard toward an alleyway between two row houses.

"It's okay, Francesca," Alex calls, shutting the metal gate behind him. "We'll get him out of here. Maybe we can talk some sense into him this time."

She doesn't thank him. She just manages a nod, and then she quickly runs down the steps to me. "Are you okay?"

My heart is pounding and my head is buzzing with everything my father said. "Why'd Alex send those guys after him?"

She reaches out to me, but I step away. "You have to trust Alex," she says. "If he can cure you, then you can be free. We just have to keep playing our cards right. Just a little longer and then—"

"Stop!" I say. I run to the gate, unlatch it, drag it open—metal grating on cement.

Alex cuts me off at the end of the alley, takes me by the shoulders, gently.

"Let him go!" I shout at Alex.

"You think he wasn't here to cause trouble? Alicia, you don't know anything about your father. We've protected you from all of that." A sad look crosses his face. "Maybe that was a mistake."

I shake him off and run into the street. The gray sky is crossed through with wires. The two guys have pushed my father into the backseat of my uncle's car. It's only now that I see they look like linebackers, not research assistants.

I wheel around and stare at my uncle. "What are you going to do with him?"

Jane walks out of the house, keys in hand.

"Jane! Tell him to let my dad go! Tell him!" I'm desperate.

She shakes her head. "Try not to worry," she says, but her voice is jangled. She's obviously shaken. "I'm sorry this had to happen, Alicia. But it's for the best. I'll see you soon." She jogs to her car.

"What the hell?" I say.

"I'm standing by this family, Alicia," Alex says, walking to the driver's seat. "If that feels unfamiliar to you, it's because your father never managed to show you how it's done." Alex gets behind the wheel.

I stand there, breathless, blood pounding in my ears.

As Alex revs the engine, I see my father through the window in the backseat. I run to him. He looks back at me, dirt on his face, worn out, but then he smiles wearily and lifts two of my pill bottles, ones he must have stolen from my coat pockets when he was hugging me, and taps them on the window as the car pulls away. I wonder for a split second if my father really wanted me to quit taking the pills or if he just wanted them for himself—a druggie and a thief.

But I know that's not right. My father came here and he told me the truth. For once, someone was telling me the truth.

CHAPTER EIGHT

WHEN THE car is out of sight, I turn around.

My mother is standing back a few feet from me, arms folded against the cold.

"He didn't do anything to me," I say. "He didn't deserve that."

"You don't understand." My mother looks so small, brittle enough to shatter. Who was she when she was with my father? Who was she when they fell in love and when they fell apart? All these years it's been easy to believe that my father was exactly what my mother and Alex had told me—maybe a good guy deep down but also the black sheep, unpredictable, crazy, a deserter. What if my mother's a liar—even if she's done it to protect me?

I squeeze my father's present in my pocket, the frayed newspaper in my grip, and I wait for her answer.

She just closes her eyes and turns away from me.

I walk to the house, leaving her standing in the yard. I throw open the front door and pass the Butlers, who are still in the living room, looking disoriented and lost.

"Party's over," I tell them. "Thanks for the five bucks." The card sits unopened on the coffee table.

I run up the stairs to my room and slam the door.

I pace around, feeling caged. I toss the present my dad gave me on the bed and stare at it.

I don't want to open it. I don't want to be disappointed, and I know the present will be disappointing.

It sits there wrapped in its wrinkled newsprint, looking sad and disappointing. I'm so used to telling myself that I don't want anything from my derelict father that I really don't want to *want to* open it, so I pretend that I don't want to.

I open the drawer on my bedside table and pull out the one picture I have of my father: I'm a three-year-old standing between him and a snowman, the snowflakes swirling around us. My father looks so much younger, not tired, not worn. His cheeks are red. He looks happy, one hand reaching down toward me; maybe he wanted to make sure I wouldn't topple over.

I put the photo back, shut the drawer, sit down on the bed, and my eyes are right back on the gift. I turn it over, slide a finger under the tape and pop it loose, then rip the newspaper.

And there is something I've seen only once before—the strangely shaped wooden cross that wasn't a cross. My father took it out after I'd been shot on the sinking cruise ship. I feel a shiver. This existed in what I thought was my twisted imagination. But here it is. I pick it up and turn it in my hands. The wood is polished. None of the ends are sharp enough to pierce the skin, but some are more pointed than others. I grip it the way he did, tightly, and it seems to fit my hand. It feels familiar. If nothing else, it's like a baton he's passed from what I thought was a fake world into my own.

If my father was telling the truth, and those other worlds I've been seeing are real, has he known me in those other worlds all these years?

And in this world, I got none of him?

And now he's gone again.

But, still, he exists in a way he hasn't ever existed before. He was worried about an atlas—a book of maps—but he also wanted me to make my own map, of what? I want to ask him, but he's gone. I feel like a hole has been punched through my heart, like I've been abandoned all over again.

And then my mother's at the door. She knocks sharply, and, as she opens the door, I put the tool in my jacket pocket with my phone. "I got called in to take a shift."

"Really?"

She looks down and I know she's lying. I'm guessing that she wants out of this house, away from me. "Then go. Take it."

She has her hand on the knob and twists it. "I know you're upset, Alicia."

"Why couldn't I see him all these years? Why did you keep him from me?"

"I've always done the best I could—"

"Please don't go into how hard it's been as a single mom. Save it for Waybourne. I want to know about my father. The truth this time."

"You know the truth. He's always been himself. He's always made things hard, and so maybe he'd have played a bigger part in your life, but we thought it was best for you not to have him around too much, not to—"

"*We* thought it was best? You and Alex? Was my father just not good enough for you? Are you embarrassed of him? Why don't you just date Alex; he's your knight in shining armor, right?"

My mother charges at me, and I think she's going to slap me.

She's never hit me before, and I kind of want her to—like leaning into the knife. *Go ahead,* I think.

But she stops short. We lock eyes and then she just turns and walks to the door. She pauses there, holding the knob again. "Don't you think I've missed him, too?"

I want to tell her that I have no idea what to think. She's never told me. But I remember how she shouted out to him to run and how he looked at her, heartbroken, refusing to. Maybe you can love someone even though you know you shouldn't.

She pulls the door shut, giving a final click.

I'm completely rattled. I pick up the tool in one hand and call Hafeez on my cell with the other.

It rings and rings, and I almost hang up because I can't even begin to figure out what to say to a machine.

Finally, he picks up and says hello, sounding groggy.

"Were you sleeping?"

"I was stealing cars," he says, meaning he's been gaming in his basement.

"My father showed up."

"On a ship this time?"

"No, real life. Backyard."

"What?"

"He got hauled off. I don't know what to do. He told me that what I've been seeing is real, Hafeez. He told me to go into the world that's cracked and dying and get this kid out. He said, 'You've been in those other worlds.' Plural, and that I can move between them."

Silence on the other end. "Hafeez?"

"No, no," he says, almost muttering to himself. "That couldn't be right. I mean, it just sounds a lot like . . ."

"Like what?"

"Um." He pauses. "I mean. Well, this is going to sound weird. . . ."

"Weirder than what I just told you?"

"Okay, okay. It sounds like the multiverse."

"The what?"

"You should pay better attention to the cooler aspects of science, you know that?"

"I have trouble translating cool, sciencewise."

"This might be some real shit, Alicia. Some really, really real shit."

"Maybe I should go after my father. Maybe I should try to find him. My mom has to have some information on him, somewhere."

"Just wait. I'm coming over. My mom took the car to play Bunco with friends. I have to ride my bike."

"My mom's going out. I could look around." My mother doesn't like me in her room. She's always said that we each needed our own space. I haven't been in her room in years, not since my last bad dream in the middle of the night. "I'm going to go dig around," I say to Hafeez. I can hear him banging around on the other end. "I should go after my father. Shouldn't I?" I stand up and hold the tool loosely. Outside it's almost dark.

"I'm running upstairs right now and I'm putting on my jacket," Hafeez says. "Do you hear me, Alicia? I'm in my garage. I'm getting my bike."

"Hurry up," I tell Hafeez.

"I'm on my way."

I stand there. I haven't even taken off my jacket. I'm just frozen, wondering what I should do. Where did they take my father? I can't just let him go—not after all this time and not after what he's just told me. It's the smallest glimpse into something much bigger.

What kind of gift is this strange object that seems to fit so perfectly in my hand?

I know the answer other people would give me: it only means my father is crazy. This is only more proof. But that doesn't work anymore. My father knew that Jax exists. It feels good to be bound in some way to Jax, but I wish I knew how we were bound and why.

In the backyard, my father said, *You ever get a feeling that there's another version of yourself? A better version, maybe?*

And I told him to shut up. Why? Because I knew exactly what he meant. One of those versions of myself got shot while trying to save a little boy from drowning in that ship. Is that what my father wanted me to understand?

I can't trust Alex anymore. I'm not even sure I can trust my mother. Maybe my father really needs me. He told me I was in danger—to get out of here. I think about slamming down the stairs and out the door to look for him, but where would I even start?

Could I really go after him?

A ridge of pain burns along my sternum again. I feel the rising pressure in my chest and reach for the pill bottles in my coat pocket but remember my father stole them. I charge toward the drawer in my bedside table for more pills, then stop.

No. My father said to stop masking the truth of who I am. Another spark of fire shoots through my chest. I straighten up, press my hands to my sternum, and fight for a breath.

I walk out of my room and to the top of the stairs, wincing from the pain, and listen for my mother. I hear her getting her coat from the front closet, grabbing her keys. The front door shuts. The car rattles to a start in the driveway.

I walk down the hall toward my mother's room. It's where she keeps all of her bills and papers. I wonder if there's anything she kept, even just to remember my father, something that could be a clue to where he is now, or at least where he's been.

I turn the knob on her bedroom door. It's locked, and suddenly I know what I want is in her room.

The house is old. The doorknob has a small hole in the center of it. I once locked myself out of my own bedroom because I'd locked the door to let my hamster roam free. My mother picked the lock with a bobby pin.

I run to the bathroom and yank open one of the drawers under the sink. Behind toothpaste, lotions, and brushes, there's a jar of bobby pins. I pick one up and run back to her door.

I kneel down and start fiddling. It takes longer than I expect, lots of blind twisting and clicking and then, finally, a little pop.

I open the door.

The room smells like her—lilac powder and hair spray. This is her private space. I feel like I'm betraying her trust just by walking in it, but my father isn't the person she led me to believe he was. Isn't that a betrayal, too? I feel guilty but also wronged.

I can't go after my father. But I can't just let him go, either.

The pain flares up my chest.

I look at the window's glassy panes growing dark, and I think of Jax in the decaying world at that camp with the quarantine sign. My father thinks I need him for some reason.

I walk to my mother's desk, cluttered with bills. I riffle through the stacks on top. I go through the top drawer, listening for any creak on the stairs.

And then I feel the sharp edge of a box. I pull it out, flip open the lid, and there's a stack of old envelopes, marked with red postal stamps, dating back years.

They're all stuffed with cash.

It's a lot of money.

Years of it. I think of not being able to pay the heating bill or for swim lessons or T-ball dues. We had the money all along.

All of the envelopes have the same return address in Jamaica Plain, a sticky label that you get from insurance company promotions.

My chest feels like it's caught fire. Is this where my father lives? Am I going after him? Is that the decision I have to make? I can barely breathe.

I take the cash from a few envelopes in the back of the box and shove it in my wallet. It was for me, anyway; I tell myself this but I don't feel convinced.

I take one envelope too, so I have the address.

Everything feels balanced on a knife edge. The pressure in my chest is explosive.

I open one more drawer. It's so light that it opens easily—only one thing skids across the bottom of the drawer. And I know it's a gun before I even see it clearly.

My mother has a gun? Is it because of the break-ins on this street? An older woman was raped just one block over this summer. Or was my mother really afraid of my father?

I think about reaching for it. Maybe, if I really go after my father, I'll need it. But I know nothing about guns. I don't even know how to check if it's loaded.

The pain's so fierce that I grunt each breath.

I could close the drawer with the gun still in it and walk back to my bedroom, take a pill, and lie back on my bed and be the person I've always been. Part of me wants to believe my mother, wants to go back to my life. Hallucinations are something I understand. My father being someone who gave up on us, who ran off, who's not right in the head is something I've learned to accept. I can pretend none of this happened. I can turn back right now and live the life I've always known.

Or I could take the gun and shove it deep into my jacket pocket with some of the cash, walk down the stairs, out the door. I can leave here and try to find my father, figure out who I really am, not the story that's been handed over.

The ripping sensation in my chest is so sharp and searing it feels almost surgical. My vision tightens on the specks of dust rotating in the fading light.

My mother's bedposts tilt. A mirror on the far wall ripples as if it were made of water.

I reach for the bedside table but miss and hit the small round box that holds my mother's lilac powder.

The box falls.

It seems to fall and fall and finally it hits the wood floor.

An explosion of white.

A powdery blizzard rising, drifting.

Snow, a storm of it.

My eyes lock onto the fine powdery flecks of my mother's powder spinning in the gray light from the windows, as I think: *Take the gun and go? Or put it back and stay?*

With shoes snow-dusted with my mother's powder, I reach for the gun, and in that moment my vision doubles, my chest convulses, and then it's as if I'm tearing from deep within, a shuddering I want to bear down on, but I have no leverage, can't scream, can't breathe.

My ribs are being pulled apart as if each is its own cage.

It's not just that my vision and my own body feel like they're blurred and doubling, but the room also seems to double. It's like my entire self is splitting and dividing.

I have a flashing fear of never belonging anywhere, being insane and cut off—forever.

The pressure in my chest grows and grows until, finally, with a

fiery pain that shoots through the center of my body, I feel myself
tearing. I've never been so stricken with terror in my life. But I give
in to it. I will either live or die, but I can't fight it any more. Gasping,
grasping for something to hold on to, I reach for the gun again, its
cold weight in my hand.

I see two slanted bedside tables and in one of them, there's another gun—just like the one I'm holding.

And then I see myself closing the drawer of the other desk, leaving the gun behind. My mother's bedroom heaves farther from the
one I'm standing in. I watch myself in that other bedroom, now
separate from this one, arching and pulling away from me. I watch
myself stagger but I don't fall. I walk quickly out of my mother's
bedroom, back down the hall to my own.

And yet I'm still myself, standing there in my mother's bedroom,
the gun heavy in my hand. I shove it into my jacket pocket, alongside my phone and the tool.

Something's going to happen to you, my father said. *When it does,
you'll know it.*

This bedroom snaps into focus as if soldered at its edges and seal-
ing itself up.

Now this is the only room.

I'm the only person here.

There's no pressure in my chest. It's gone. There's only a dull
ache in the lower part of my ribs on one side of my body, more like
the memory of pain than real pain.

I'm shaking but I feel relieved—like I'm on the other side of it all.

Is it possible that this is what I've been waiting for without knowing I was waiting for anything at all? And then I know one thing
that is absolutely true: this was what my father was talking about.
He said I'd know when it happened, and I do. I feel different, and

even though I've just gone through something surreal and otherworldly, I feel stronger, more sure of myself. Actually, more *myself.*

Spandrel. My father told me that's what I am. The word comes back to me now, strange and beautiful. But I still don't know what it means.

I walk out of my mother's bedroom into the hall.

I look into my own bedroom. It's empty.

I run down the hall, down the stairs.

There's my leftover cake from the party, plastic-wrapped within an inch of its life, sitting on the kitchen counter.

This is our house. There's nothing strange about it. This is the house we've always lived in. For so long I've thought my mother and I only had each other. That was a lie.

I open the front door and close it quietly behind myself.

Breathing the cold air, I can sense the other me—the one who put the gun back and is now standing in her bedroom as if she's real.

But she feels very real.

It's like I know the other me is dazed, pacing slowly in her bedroom, trying to make sense of what's just happened. She's on the phone, probably calling Hafeez again, to see if he's on the way.

But I'm standing here in my yard, a gun in one of my jacket pockets.

I look up at my bedroom window.

I'm not there.

I'm here, out in the cold almost-dark.

I turn to go, and there, at the end of the street, Hafeez rounds the corner, pedaling his bike toward me.

CHAPTER NINE

THE WIND is sharp and cold. My ribs feel all cinched up. Hafeez is walking his bike alongside me, and I'm trying to explain everything that just happened, but I know it's coming out fast and jumbled. "I don't really get any of it. I only know what I feel. And I felt the worlds rip in two. *I* ripped in two. The other me—I know she's kept going."

Hafeez only nods, trying not to interrupt. Once we've made it to the bus stop, I lean against the sign's metal post.

"And what's this other you doing now?" He still has a fat lip from taking Sprowitz's punch, so his words come out in a mumble.

I can see my other self in my head. "She's wearing sweatpants and a sweatshirt and she's talking to you in her room. You came over."

Hafeez looks at me, surprised.

She's kind of becoming someone else in this moment, just slightly. I can feel the difference like it's a tiny crack in the surface of a frozen lake. She made a different decision. She's becoming the person who didn't take the gun, who didn't go after her father. Her choice is shaping her, not the other way around. "She's not me anymore,"

I tell Hafeez, who's bent over, locking his bike to a parking sign. "I took the gun. She didn't. We're becoming different people."

Hafeez straightens up. "What? You have . . ." He lowers his voice and leans toward me. "You have *a gun?*"

I nod.

"Jesus! Why?" Then he mutters to himself, "This is not good. This is *not good!*"

"I thought it would make me feel safer."

"It doesn't make *me* feel safer!" Hafeez's eyes are wide.

The gun doesn't make me feel any safer, either—if anything it feels risky, like it could turn on me. "I don't even know how to shoot a gun." I see the lights of the bus turn the corner, headed toward us. "What are we doing, Hafeez? I can't find my father! What if this address is old and he doesn't live there anymore?"

"Look, it's all we have. It's a start."

"It's not all we have." I pull out the tool and show it to Hafeez.

"What is it?" he says.

"I have no idea. But I've seen it in that hallucination, the one with my father on the sinking cruise ship."

"What was he doing with it?"

"I don't know. I'd just gotten shot. It's all a little blurry. It was in his hand, though. I know it was."

The bus groans to a stop in front of us.

I slip the tool back into my pocket. The bus door opens but neither of us moves toward it. We're both a little dazed.

"In or out?" the driver says. "What'll it be?"

"In." Hafeez nudges me toward the bus. "Definitely in."

There are only a few passengers, bundled and hunched in their coats. Their faces are cast in a greenish hue from the dull overhead lights.

As I follow Hafeez down the aisle, I feel the gun's heaviness in my jacket pocket. And I feel dangerous, kind of powerful and scared at the same time.

Hafeez and I slide into a seat. He asks for the tool and I hand it over.

He studies it for a few minutes and then stares at me intensely. "You trust him, right?"

I've never trusted my father. He couldn't even do the simplest part of being a father: showing up. But now everything's changed. He was there. I saw him with my own eyes. He was *fatherly.* "I think he was telling me the truth, or trying to." I nod. "Yes. I trust him. I have to." It feels foreign to trust my father, but hopeful too. "I mean, I'm hoping I might not be crazy after all."

"And he knew the poem, too. How did it go?"

" *'I am, I am, I am.'* And then he added, *You are, you are, you are.*"

"Couldn't that be about the multiverse? That there are different versions of each of you?"

My father said that he kept one version of himself hidden—the good one. . . . "I guess so."

He hands me the tool and pulls out his phone. " 'Spandrel,' that's the word your father used, right?"

"Right."

He clicks around and then says, "Okay. There's an architectural definition of spandrel. It's like the leftover space in a building. For example, the triangular curved area between arches or the space under a set of stairs. The by-products." He opens a few more searches. "Here's a definition in poetry. Some guy named Giampietro invented a kind of poem called a spandrel that uses leftover pieces cut from poems to make new poems."

"Did Plath write spandrels?" I wonder aloud.

"Probably not. She was dead before Giampietro was born." He keeps clicking. "Wait. What's this?"

I lean toward his phone.

"This one's the gold mine. Looks like Stephen J. Gould and some guy named Lewontin applied the term to evolutionary biology. According to Wikipedia Gould and Lewontin believe that a spandrel is 'any biological feature of an organism that arises as a necessary side consequence of other features, which is not directly selected for by natural selection.' Again, the by-products."

I shake my head. "And that's a gold mine *because* . . ."

Hafeez folds his arms on his chest, and, in a professorial way, he taps his chin. "Is this weird thing that's happening to you genetic or something? If language is a by-product of evolution, this weirdness could be, too. Maybe a bunch of people are out there going through this. It could have been handed down from your father."

"I've inherited the ability to move through universes?"

"Tell me what happened. Start at the beginning."

I replay the whole scene at the party for him, slower and calmer this time. I start with the shock of seeing my father and I try to remember everything he said about worlds and versions of yourself. And I tell Hafeez about the world my father wanted me to go into, the one that's dying. "He talked about this kid named Jax, and how he wanted me to help get Jax out of that world. And I know who Jax is. I've seen him. And he wanted me to tell Jax's mother to go get the atlas, if the world was going to die, that he probably wouldn't be able to help. But I can't tell her." I don't mention to Hafeez that I can't stop thinking about Jax. I'm not ready to say it out loud, and part of me knows it might hurt Hafeez.

"Jax's mother is dead. And my father told me I can't trust Alex and that he never stole from him, but Alex thinks he did." And then I describe my parents together, seeing them like that for the first time, the way they looked at each other. And how it all fell apart—Alex's research assistants dragging my father away.

"And then there's Jane." I go back over the conversation I overheard in her office and how she left the party as soon as she could. "'I'm sorry *this* had to happen.' She said it like she knew something was going to happen and the problem was bad timing."

Hafeez is staring out the window, watching the city glide by, but I know he's listening.

"All this time she and Alex have been upping my meds," I tell him, "when maybe all I needed was whatever happened to me in my mother's room."

"What was it like?" he asks.

"It was like being torn in half, of being two people, not just one, but I'm glad it happened. Did you see how I got on the bus? No hesitation, no freak-out. The panic over every small decision—it's gone." I got over something when I took the gun—and at the same time put it back and went to my bedroom. I see my other self, again, back at home—an image as vivid as any of my hallucinations. She's lying on her back, the pieces of her notebook all torn up around her. She's given up and she's scared too. I tell Hafeez about it. "Why am I still seeing this other version of myself?"

"When we went back to Pakistan one summer for a month," Hafeez says, "my mother kept saying, 'This is the life we left behind. This is what I would have been doing. This is where we would have been living.' It was like she was seeing an alternate universe. Maybe she was seeing some version of a universe that was real in some way."

We switch over to the T, taking the line that goes toward Forest Hills. He asks me about the poem with the lines "I am, I am, I am." "What's the title?"

" 'Suicide off Egg Rock.' "

"That's grim."

"Well, you know how Plath died, right?"

He nods.

"There is no line 'You are, you are, you are.' "

"What's the poem about?"

"It's a little blurry. It's more a feeling of complete desperation."

He searches the poem on his phone, and we start to skim it to-gether.

And then we both stop reading at the same line. "It's about a tattoo, how the blood beats it," I say.

"Your dad's tattoo," Hafeez says. "Do you think he's trying to make a point?"

I shrug. "He didn't have much time. He had so much to say that it was all compressed." I rub my temples. "Like the cracked world, the one I'm supposed to go into and save Jax and maybe some atlas he was worried about too? I don't even really know Jax." I sigh. "Are we getting anywhere?"

"Well, only literally. I mean, we're here," Hafeez says.

And we are—the second to last stop at Green Street in Jamaica Plain.

We shuffle off the train, back out into the ripping cold.

There's a Bikes Not Bombs bike shop, a ball field dusted with snow. I pull the envelope out of my jacket pocket, and Hafeez looks up the address.

As we head down Seaverns toward Centre Street, I say, "Do you think my father was trying to talk to me through a Plath poem? Who does that?"

"My father would have left me a complex chemistry equation."

"But, Hafeez, I'm not just crazier than ever, am I? I mean, I'm not falling into some deeper well of my father's craziness. You'd tell me if you thought I'd lost it, wouldn't you?"

He nods. "I would. I think I have in the past, right?"

"True."

I stop walking. I'm struck by a memory—or at least that's how it feels: my father helping me start up a handmade go-cart on a boardwalk in winter. At first the engine revved, then stalled, revved and stalled again. But finally he got it going, and as I zipped down the windy boardwalk, gray clouds were passing quickly across the sky, and my father was jumping and laughing and cheering.

"What's wrong?" Hafeez asks.

"Nothing." I'm not sure what to say—I'm having a memory of something I've never remembered before? And it's such a simple, little, sweet scene. Did it happen?

At the Purple Cactus, we take a left on Centre, and, after a few blocks, we come to South Street. My face has tightened up from the cold. My toes are numb.

"Is there a universe where Hitler made it as an artist instead of a dictator?" I ask.

"Is there one where Abe Lincoln couldn't pull it off? Where the states are all chopped up like Europe?"

"And Gandhi," I say. "He couldn't have prevailed in most universes. I mean, the decks were stacked against him."

"I wonder if there's a version of myself who can ask a girl out, you know?" Hafeez says, stuffing his hands into his jacket pockets.

"I wonder if there's a version of me where I have my shit together," I say.

The wind is so sharp, it stings my face.

"The other you?" Hafeez asks. "Can you tell what she's doing now? Is she still freaking out?"

I stop walking and think about it for a minute. "She's talking to you," I say. "I guess both versions of me rely on you. By the way, thank you for taking that punch."

"That's okay. I'd do it again."

"I hope you don't have to."

It's quiet for a minute or two, and then I say, "For the first time in a long time, I'm moving toward something, Hafeez."

He looks at me and smiles in that bemused way of his. "Me too."

CHAPTER TEN

MY FATHER'S apartment building is a shit-hole. The lobby is small and dirty. Empty milk cartons are flattened in one corner. Take-out fliers litter the ground near the wall of mailboxes. There's a small desk, as if there used to be a doorman. But no one's around. No security either. No way to buzz anyone up.

I'm embarrassed by it and I feel guilty for being embarrassed. He's my father. He isn't rich. So what?

"Are you sure this is it?" Hafeez says. Maybe he wants to turn back. Part of me would like to.

"I'm sure."

We walk to the elevators and push the up arrow.

"I hope they regularly inspect these things," Hafeez says. "It's a state law, right?"

Once inside the elevator, Hafeez immediately checks the little placard with the last inspection date. Before the doors shut, I put my arm out and say, "Let's take the stairs."

The stairs have their own stench, the sickly sweet smell of rot.

We jog up them fast and open the door to a long hallway, lit by a single bulb. My father's apartment is 3F, at the end.

"What if they roughed him up and dropped him off?" I say. "What if he's here?"

"That would be weird," Hafeez says. "Why not try to stay in touch with you? Why not just give you a phone number?"

I stop a few feet from his door. "Was Alex going to try to talk him into some kind of rehab? This is the kind of place where an addict would live. Isn't it?"

"God, I hope we're not tracking down a meth head."

I whip around. "You said you'd tell me if you thought I was crazy."

"Yeah, but who's going to tell me if I'm crazy, too?"

"Shit."

I close my eyes. I try to remember the moment when my father hugged me and I knew he was speaking the truth. I try to hold on to that now.

I raise my knuckles to the door, take a breath. For a second, I wonder if my father has another wife, another daughter, an entire other life, all on the other side of this door. I steel myself and knock.

"Nice decision-making," Hafeez whispers. "Sans freak-out."

"Nice use of random French."

He's right. No panic, no feeling of my chest ripping in half.

We wait.

Nothing.

I knock again.

No voices, no footsteps. No other family. In fact, no one.

"Try the knob," Hafeez says.

"You try it."

He reaches forward, twists the knob, and we're both expecting it to be locked, but it isn't. The door swings open. The weak hallway light spills a yellow rectangle around my shadow.

I flip the light switch, not expecting it to work, but it does. Hafeez locks the door behind us. I slip my hand around the gun in my pocket.

The apartment is almost completely empty. Nothing on the walls. A kitchen to the left, beyond that, a hallway. The only furniture in the living room is a sofa—an old one that reminds me of the Butlers' house, the couch Arnie sleeps on and stinks up.

We step inside. "Hello?"

"He's not here," Hafeez says. "And this *might* be a criminal offense. Breaking and entering."

"It's my dad's place. I'm supposed to enter."

The dining room has an old table with two mismatched chairs.

The bedroom has a well-made bed, a dark blue blanket, one pillow.

Is this all my father owns in the world? I shake my head, wide-eyed. I'm suddenly afraid I might choke up. It's that depressing.

Hafeez opens the closet—two white shirts and two pairs of pants hung on metal wires. No shoes.

He's about to say something but then looks at me and reads my expression. I must look fragile, because he says, "I'll give you a minute," and he walks back to the front door.

In the bathroom, the regular stuff—a toothbrush, razor, shampoo, soap. I pick up my father's toothbrush and push the brush onto the back of my hand—dry. The soap too. He hasn't been here for a while.

I think of what my father said, that I would find out he's not a stranger after all. How am I ever going to find that out if I never see him again?

What will I do now? Go home? Back to my old life and wait—for what? To get dropped into the Freaks Track for the rest of high school? I'll have brought Hafeez all the way out here for what? A dead end.

I can't give up. There has to be something. I'm angry at my father now—like it's his fault I'm here in the first place, and it is.

I walk back to the living room. "Why'd he show up at all?" I say to Hafeez. "Just to mess with me?"

I flip up the sofa cushions. Nothing. Not even spare change.

"He could've just left me alone. I would have figured out how to survive. I was surviving, right?"

"Are you okay?" Hafeez says.

I'm not okay. I storm into the kitchen. No food in the fridge. I yank open drawer after empty drawer.

And then one drawer isn't empty. There's an old newspaper, and when I pick it up, a pair of heavy scissors falls, stabbing the floor. I spread the paper out and find that the comics have been cut. "Did he wrap my present with this?"

Hafeez is a little afraid of me right now. "Maybe we should go," he says quietly.

I open a few more empty drawers and then find one holding a bunch of battered pocket-size foreign-language phrase books, including one for Ukrainian and one for Russian.

I lift the Ukrainian one and show it to Hafeez. "What the hell?" I say. I turn a few pages. They're rippled as if they were once soaked through. "Look! The Dnieper flows through the Ukraine. The book could fit in a pocket."

"Wow," Hafeez says, impressed and also a little scared.

I open cupboards and find three tins marked FLOUR, OATS, SUGAR. I pop them open, one by one. The sugar and oats tins are empty, but the flour tin has sugar in it—and weevils, dark and curled.

I shake the tin, and then see a white sharp edge. I tilt the sugar tin over the sink, letting some of the sugar fall into the basin. "Come here," I tell Hafeez.

We both look into the canister. I reach in and pull out some photos. They're faded Instamatic pictures of my father and me—typical childhood shots.

"That's you," Hafeez says. "How old?"

"Old enough to remember these places, being with my father, but I don't."

In one, I'm about six and I'm cradling a puppy. A bulldog. "In one of the worlds, there's an ancient bulldog. Could it be the same dog?"

I don't wait for an answer. I flip to the next picture. I'm having a birthday party, poolside with palm trees around it, and bright balloons. I must be eight or so. I'm opening presents surrounded by kids and a few adults, all strangers to me. Is this somewhere balmy? "My birthday's in February."

"Nice place," Hafeez says.

"It'd be nicer if I remembered it."

One of the kids is staring straight at the camera, and I feel like I can almost remember him, but he's smiling so hard that his face is distorted, his eyes squinched up too tightly. I should remember all of these people. I can't explain how it makes me feel—lost, nostalgic, but without a real place or time or people to grab hold of. The loss of it all crashes into me.

Then I see my father in the background wearing short sleeves, and, for the first time, I can make out the more elaborate tattoos, the vines and branches and small leaves that snake asymmetrically up both of his arms.

I look around the kitchen—linoleum coming loose at one edge, rust spot in the sink. The fridge rattles on.

"These pictures are proof," Hafeez says, "that those worlds are real."

"I didn't have the hallucinations until the past year or so. But I existed in these worlds as a kid. I was there with my father. How is it possible?"

And then I turn to the final picture—which is almost an exact copy of the photo I have in my bedroom—the two of us making a snowman, the flakes swirling around us. In this one, my father isn't looking at the camera, though. He's looking at me. It must have been taken just seconds before or after the one I have in my bedside table.

I look out the dark windows of my father's apartment and then pull out my phone. "Should I call Jane?"

"I don't know. It might be—"

"Dangerous, I know."

"All this time she's been upping your meds, and she had to know, right?"

"Like you said, 'These pictures are proof.' I know I can't trust her, but I don't know what else to do." I look at Hafeez, waiting for his answer.

He nods. "Yeah. Go ahead."

I press the call button.

As soon as her line starts ringing, I realize she could be getting ready for bed. But I don't care.

She picks up, and her voice is alert, like she sits up nights waiting for calls from patients who've lost their minds. "Hello?"

"It's Alicia."

"Are you okay?"

I pace a small circle. "No. You should have told me. Why didn't you?"

"Where are you?" Does she already know I took off? My mother wouldn't have known unless she came home early from work. Maybe Alex had someone check up on me and he called Jane. Maybe she *was* sitting up waiting for a call from a patient who'd lost her mind.

"I'm at my father's apartment looking at the most messed-up family photo album in the history of family photo albums."

"Let me come and get you. You're upset. You need help. Are you still in Jamaica Plain?"

I stop. "You know where my father lives?" I look at Hafeez. Of course she does.

"What?"

"I didn't tell you where his apartment was."

"Of course you did. How else would I know?"

But I didn't.

"You need help, Alicia. Listen to me. You have to—"

My arm goes slack. I click the phone shut. I can feel the expanse of lies opening like a canyon at my feet.

"Let's get out of here," Hafeez says.

I slip the photographs in my empty jacket pocket. They belong to my father, and I shouldn't even be here, but I won't give them up.

We walk out of the apartment and shut the door. The hallway carpet smells sharply of mildew. Down the hall, someone's listening to a football game.

The lights flicker, dim, flicker. We take the stairs.

Maybe I'm not right in the head after all. Maybe this isn't reality, just a deeper layer of crazy, a craziness that's been amping up in me all my life.

I speed up on the stairs, sprint through the dark lobby.

Behind me, Hafeez says, "Wait up!"

I burst out of the apartment's lobby doors.

It's started snowing.

The phone starts ringing. I look at it—Jane. I don't answer.

The flakes are small and quick. I start walking, fast. Hafeez catches up. I wonder if I'm going to get sick.

Hafeez says, "I don't know what we should do now. I wish I did. Maybe we should go home."

"I can't go home."

And then—out of nowhere—I have another memory. My father holding a stick with a butterfly, completely still, perched on it. "A butterfly can flap its wings in one world," he says, "and because we've opened doors and windows between worlds, the beating of its wings can cause a storm somewhere else altogether. You know what I'm saying, Alicia? Do you understand?" I was just a little kid. The sun was warm on my head. The butterfly opened its wings and flew off.

Did I understand?

"What if these memories have always been in my head, just hidden, the way the Butlers wrapped up their chairs and sofas in white sheets when they tried to go live with their alcoholic son for a while. Maybe I've always known that something was there—draped in bedsheets—and I just didn't know to lift the sheets and look."

"It's not time travel," Hafeez says, clapping his hands together to keep warm. "But it is moving between realities. I swear this is the stuff that physicists my dad knows can only whisper to each other about at backyard barbecues after they've had some beer, because no one would believe them. But they know it's all theoretically possible."

I stare at Hafeez. "What physicists whisper to each other at backyard barbecues? How is that going to help me? In my present situation. I'm asking you, Hafeez. How is that relevant?"

"You could test it."

"Test what?"

"Try going into your other world, the one where you didn't take the gun. I think it would be worth an experiment."

The idea feels huge and powerful and terrifying. "Last time I had an attack of decision-making, I poked my hand with a compass."

"You did what?"

"I had this theory about blood. Every time I had really moved into one of my father's worlds, I had cut myself or saw blood from some imagery—like your fat lip. So I set it up."

He touches his lip. "And?"

"It worked."

I turn down an alley and lean against the side of a brick building. "But since I took the gun, I haven't been anxious about a decision." It figures—now that I want an attack, I'm no longer able to have one.

"Maybe you don't need those panic attacks anymore."

"Jane always asked me what it felt like in my body when the hallucinations came on. The ripping feeling in my chest, the aches all over my body. If I applied pressure, I would sometimes fade out faster."

"That sounds easier than drawing blood, right? I'd rather not take another blow to the face. Try the pressure thing. I'll be right here."

"Okay."

I decide to squeeze the back of my neck. Nothing. I hold on to my arm, where Hafeez grabbed me when I lost it in the cafeteria. I tighten my grip.

Nothing.

I apply pressure to my collarbone.

Still nothing.

My phone rings again.

"Jane," I tell Hafeez. I take a look and I'm right. I've got to get rid of this phone. In one quick motion, I spike it and watch it bounce and splinter.

"Was that necessary?"

"I'm pretty sure it was. Plus, it felt good." I look up at the snow, coming down quick. I lean against the brick wall again and close my eyes.

"I have whole childhoods with my father." My knees feel weak. I sit on the ground and bang my back against the bricks. "What if my father didn't abandon me in any world except this one?"

Hafeez sits down next to me. "It's going to be okay, Alicia."

"Are you sure about that?"

"Not absolutely."

Staring at the snow spinning against the sky, it reminds me of my mother's powder, the flecks of it that I saw when the room started to double. I feel that deep painful buzz again, but this time it isn't in my arm or neck or collarbone. It's in the back of my rib cage in the spot where, after things doubled and ripped in two in my mother's bedroom, there was just that strange dull ache. Now it's almost as if my ribs are shivering beneath my skin.

I want to hurl myself into the pain. This is it!

I curl forward and push against the brick, applying pressure to the back of my ribs.

"What's wrong?" Hafeez says.

"Shhh."

Slowly, everything shifts to points; each snowflake catches on the brick building, and it's as if the bricks are being snagged and pulled apart by the snowflakes. The snowflakes start dragging pieces of the brick and sky as they pivot in the wind, leaving behind pieces of nothingness—a black, whistling void.

My vision darkens like I'm going to pass out. "I'm either going into another world or I'm going to die in this shit part of town."

The thought echoes and echoes.

Then there's nothing. And it is like I have died. The world is still and silent and gray. . . .

. . . Tick, tick, and hissing.

The radiator in my bedroom. It's night, as dark outside the windows as it was outside of my dad's apartment building, but I'm in my sweatpants and a sweatshirt, holding the tool my father gave me.

And there's Hafeez. He's looking at me intently.

Something's happened. He's waiting for a response.

"Well?" he says nervously. "Say something. Anything."

The room feels electrically charged. I don't know what moment I've slipped into, but a lot is at stake.

"What's happening?"

"What do you mean? I just asked you . . . a question and . . . are you okay?"

"I'm not me," I whisper quickly. "I called you? You came over, right? And we've been in this room, and I told you about, about—"

"I came over, and you were crying, and you told me what happened in your mother's room. You said—"

"I said that everything ripped in half and there were two worlds, two of me. And one of me took the gun and left, and that one met you as you were riding your bike around the corner."

"What?" Hafeez says.

And I feel like my voice isn't mine either. It's just slightly off. I'm aware of the scratchiness of it because of all the crying. "I'm the one who took the gun."

Hafeez isn't sure what to think. I can tell he's a little doubtful, like maybe he's wondering if I'm just trying to get out of whatever it is I'm supposed to be saying—whatever this something, anything, is. "Are you serious?" he says.

I nod. "After we met up, we went to my father's address, his shitty apartment, and I found photographs of my childhoods. My other childhoods."

I can tell he's trying to change gears.

He grabs his head and holds it for a second, just trying to line everything up. "So you don't know what happened here. You don't remember . . . how upset you were and how we . . ."

"How we what?" But then I know. We kissed.

He blushes and smiles and shakes his head. "Nothing," he says. "I mean. If you don't know, I shouldn't say anything." And I know that I'm a different person here. I'm the kind of person who decided to go back to the life handed to her. I felt guilty and I wanted to be told it wasn't that bad, that I was going to be alright. And Hafeez did tell me those things, and I must have liked that part of him, too.

"Have you figured out anything here, from her side of things?" I ask, trying to change the subject.

"Well, one thing: 'Suicide off Egg Rock,'" he says. They must have looked it up in this world, too. He pulls out his phone as if he's about to start reading it aloud. I stop him. "We've talked about that poem too, the tattoos in it. Maybe my dad wanted us to look up that poem, and to start thinking about the tattoos as more than just tattoos, right?"

"Yeah," Hafeez says.

"I've seen the tattoos on my dad's wrists and on his neck, too, little vines and branches. Maybe his ink runs all over his arms and shoulders. All over his body even."

"The buzzing all over your body before you move into another . . . world. The tattoos all over his. It can't be a coincidence. We're trying to figure it out."

"Good," I say, for the first time thinking having two of me and Hafeez might mean we can divide and conquer. "Keep working on that."

I move to my window. It's snowing, the same light dusty flakes that were floating down outside of my father's apartment. But what does that mean? Nothing. It's *now* here and it's *now* there.

My mother's car is gone. The street is empty. Not even Sprowitz eyeing me.

"I have to go."

"What? Where?" Hafeez says.

"Back to myself. Back to the other me." I walk out of the bedroom, and Hafeez follows me as I walk to my mother's bedroom.

Hafeez stands in the doorway. "C'mon," he says. "This is beyond anything I've ever imagined. Don't you see what could potentially be going on here?"

I smell my mother's lilac powder and hair spray again. "I have no idea what could be potentially be going on here, Hafeez." I walk to the bedside table, open the drawer.

The gun is still there.

I shut the drawer, walk back out of the room past Hafeez, and head down the stairs.

"It's amazing, Alicia. You're moving through space and time and universes!" he says as he follows me out the front door, down the stoop, and onto the narrow driveway.

"Yes, but the question is how do I do it? Any thoughts on that?"

"Mr. Javits didn't get to parallel universes in Intro to Physics." He's only wearing thick socks, so he's shifting from foot to foot. "Look," he says, "about what I asked you in there when you showed up."

"That's between you and her, Hafeez. I'm not her anymore."

"Yeah, but I feel like I should back up and, I don't know . . ."

Part of me knows what happened in there. We kissed, and Hafeez wanted to know what it meant. I can almost remember it like it happened to me. Maybe I have had a crush on Hafeez, too, but not now. I don't even know who I am anymore. But the other me? The one who put the gun back? "Ask her again," I say. "Whatever it was."

"You think I should?" he says, and now it's like he's asking the best friend of the girl he likes. It's all shifting.

"Yeah," I say, "I've got to go."

"What are you going to do?"

"Take the advice of another you and experiment." I reach around my back and push on my ribs and hold my breath, trying to get back to that moment. It worked before. Maybe it will work again, take me back to myself—in the alley. I want to understand this. I need to have some kind of control.

A dog's barking in the distance; a siren is tapering off down another street. I keep holding my breath and pushing on the ribs in my lower back.

"Alicia," Hafeez says. "What are you doing?"

I hear a dull ringing in my ears. The noises fade. The snow doesn't snag or pull anything.

Still, my vision bleeds to black.

I start to stagger.

When I come to, I'm lying flat on my back in my driveway. I can see the curled toes of Hafeez's socks.

"What the hell?" Hafeez is saying, tugging on my arm and petting my shoulder. "You're bleeding!" He's trying to help me sit up.

The thin layer of snow on the ground around me is tinged pink. My chin aches. I touch it, and my fingers come away wet with blood. I didn't need blood to get into this world, the one I created, but it got me into all of those other worlds with my father. And pressure on my ribs got me here, but maybe it's not pressure in my ribs that will take me back.

"You're going to need stitches for that," Hafeez says. "I'll drive you."

"No, this is what I need." I hear the dog, still barking. A car passes by. A neighbor's light across the street goes dark.

"What are you talking about? Come inside."

In the glow of the streetlight, I see the fine delicate laciness of the snow, the light steam coming off the blood and my breath.

"Come on!" Hafeez says. "Let's get a compress on it. It's wicked cold out here. Aren't you freezing?"

I shake my head and it feels heavy. The pain zeros in on my upper arm, a fiery pain shooting through it. I grab it and press hard. The snowflakes become moving points of light. Everything shifts, even Hafeez—his face clouded with confusion. I'm fading and the cold burrows deep. . . .

. . . My ribs are vibrating, pressed against the metal interior of a delivery truck of some sort of—midsize moving van? It's packed with people and their suitcases, dark except for a few flashlights.

The old man is beside me, the bulldog on his lap, and I'm holding a different beat-up copy of Sylvia Plath's *The Collected Poems*. The cover is cracked and torn so that I can only see half of the black-and-white photograph of her face. I love her poems in every world, I guess.

"Gemmy," I whisper. I don't waste any time. "I talked to my dad. I'm here from another branch. Do you know what I'm saying? Who am I in this world?"

Gemmy dips closer to my face. His eyes fill with tears. He tries to say something but his throat tightens. He coughs and tries again. "Jesus, Alicia. It's me." He grips my hands.

"How do I know you?"

"I'm your old man's old man," he whispers, smoothing his fine gray hairs.

Gemmy—I remember: it's how I pronounced "Grandpa" as a toddler. "But you're dead."

He smiles wide. "Not in this branch. Some cats have nine lives, some have even more." He looks down the row of people—sleeping or dazed and staring off. A few kids are curled on their parents' laps. "We're like family. There's all kinds of ways to be family. You and I got more than one."

He wraps his arm around me. I give in to it and hug him tight. This is Gemmy, my grandfather. He was dead but he's somehow alive. I smell his talc and the faint scent of liquor. This is what grandfathers smell like, I think. Everybody deserves a grandfather. My eyes sting with tears.

"You're my kiddo. We've had a lot of good times, you and me. We're buddies, you know."

I don't know, but I can feel it. "I'm so glad you're alive," I say. "I'm so glad you're *here*."

"Good Lord," Gemmy says, bright-eyed and breathless. "The time has really come. Been a long wait. I'll have to get the families together. You're the next generation, Alicia." He claps me on the shoulder. "You'll be the one to fix this mess. I can feel it."

"Fix what? I can't fix anything. I don't even understand—" I want to say more, but the pains zing throughout my body and land on my clavicle. I grab my collarbone. The truck engine growls louder and louder. He's talking to me, but I can't hear anything but the roaring engine. Bodies bobble and then break apart. . . .

. . . I'm find myself paused on a set of stairs, gripping a glossy wooden banister. A man's voice upstairs shouts instructions to find a certain pill bottle on the coffee table in the living room.

"Okay!" I call back to him.

My mother is dying.

Jax exists here. His mother is already dead. When he handed me the weeds by the chain-link fence surrounding the quarantine camp, he said to tell my father that he needed to be looking into those seeds disappearing into thin air, that this is all going to go away. Everything. This whole splintering, cracked, disintegrating world.

Is my father even in this branch? I've always known if he was nearby. But I have no feeling for him at all. Nothing.

And there before me is a marble mantel, fireplace, and, above it all, a painting of a family—a mother, a father, a girl about eight years old or so.

The mother is my mother.

The girl is me.

But the father isn't my father.

The father is Uncle Alex.

My mother's hair is swept up in a loose bun. She's wearing a gauzy blouse. Someone's put me in a dress with a lace collar, and my bangs look freshly trimmed. Alex wears a blue blazer. We're all stiff-backed and smiling just enough to make our cheeks rise but not enough to show our teeth. And there's a yellow Labrador retriever with us—but that was so long ago, he must be gone.

In this world, Alex is my father?

How is that possible? I feel sick.

I see the pill bottles on the coffee table. I grab all of them. But I also see a pen and pick it up. My soul or my mind or something moves between these places, but my body stays. I don't know if it will work, but I wonder what would happen if I write myself a note. Hoping that the other Alicia, the one who finds herself in this body, will get it, I write as fast as I can on my arm: *Find Jax. Tell him there's another world and I'm in it and I'm real.*

Will this only confuse her? Will this mean anything at all? I have no idea. The back of my neck burns. I turn and head back up the steps. I run but then trip. I scramble to my feet, but the pain is so sharp that I fall to my knees . . . and the floor turns brittle. My vision is cracking. . . .

. . . My mouth is filled with blood. It's hard to breathe, like a few of my ribs are cracked. I'm on the ground. I see a pair of scuffed boots—heavy-duty, steel toed. Someone muttering above me, not in English but I understand: "What are you going to do now, you piece of shit?"

Am I back in Russia?

Like an answer, I feel the spiraling pain in my shoulder blade— the gunshot wound.

Someone's calling to him. "Iosif!" He's the one who shot me. He and his thugs kidnapped us off of the cruise ship.

I can barely move from the pain. My right hand buzzes. I grab it and hold on tight, hoping this will send me back.

Iosif leans into my face. An old scar runs jaggedly across one cheek. "What?" he asks, grinning. "You want more?"

I'm shaking my head. I hurt too much to speak. But he points a gun at my face anyway. I see his finger move, the kick of the gun, but there's no sound.

The ground falls away. . . .

. . . I'm wearing the clothes I had on when I took the gun. I check my pockets: the gun's there, the cash I took, the tool my father gave me—all of it. I'm sitting with my back against the brick wall. My jeans are dusted with snow.

I see Hafeez standing at the end of the alley in the light thrown by the streetlamp, keeping a lookout.

"How long have I been here like this?" I ask him.

"Hey," he says, jogging to me. "Not too long."

I touch my chin. "I'm not bleeding." It was never cut.

"Why would you be bleeding?"

"My ribs are fine too—not broken."

"So, I take it things aren't perfect in other worlds?" he asks.

"Nope, not perfect."

"Did you get to the world where you were asking me for help? Did I show up?"

I can't tell him about the charged air between us. I wouldn't know how. "Yep. You did."

"And, what was I like?"

"You're you," I say.

"Right. I mean, who else would I be?"

I want to tell him that we're both already different in that world, that the slight tweak of events unlocked things and changed everything completely. But I'm afraid he'll ask more questions than I want to answer.

I stand up and brush off the snow. "My body doesn't go from world to world, so what does? My soul? Some part of my mind?"

"I wish I knew."

"It worked, you know, without blood. I was looking at the snow. It reminded me of my mother's lilac powder, which was what I was focusing on when everything ripped in two in her bedroom."

"So maybe there's some sort of trigger."

"Maybe, like my father's worlds require blood but mine are different. Mine might be powder or dust or something light and spinning, like snow."

"And then there's also this trigger in your body too, right?"

"Right. A specific spot of pain."

"Mind and body triggers," he says, and I can tell his brain is whirring.

"My grandfather, Gemmy, is alive in another branch, and he's under the impression I can fix things."

"Interesting."

"And in one branch"—I don't even want to say it aloud, but I have to get it out—"my mother married my uncle. I saw us in a family portrait. But if Alex was my father, I wouldn't have my own face at all, but I did."

"Did he adopt you?"

I shrug. Every little tiny piece of information I get only makes things blurrier.

"The main thing is that it worked. You're getting better at it, right?"

We hear a car door slam at the end of the alley. We both turn.

"Maybe we should go home," Hafeez says. "We need to start over. Come at everything fresh."

"But we were going toward something for once."

"I have a chem test tomorrow and that shit has gotten real. Come

on. Come back with me." He smiles. He knows I've been through
a lot.

But then we hear a voice shout, "Hey! There you are!"

There's a figure at the end of the alley, backlit by the streetlamp.
Hafeez must have better eyesight than I do, because he says, "Holy
shit. How'd Sprowitz find us here?"

Sprowitz starts to run at us. Hafeez and I take off in the opposite
direction, but a chain-link fence blocks the end of the alley, and
Sprowitz is fast.

I sprint and jump as high as I can, gripping the links, and Hafeez
is a second later, but Sprowitz grabs the back of his jacket and pulls
him down. Hafeez lands hard, Sprowitz is leaning over him, and
I've got just one shot at this—one slim moment while Sprowitz's
back is turned—so I push off, still holding the fence, and kick him
in the back of the head.

This sends Sprowitz sprawling. Hafeez gets up, but Sprowitz
has a wrestler's quickness and tackles Hafeez, getting him in a
stranglehold. "I'm not even here for you, towelhead. What the fuck
are you doing here, anyway?" He sounds confused and angry, like if
Hafeez weren't here, he wouldn't have to hurt him. But it doesn't
stop him.

Hafeez's face flushes. "Go," he grunts at me. "Run."

I can't leave him. I reach into my pocket, slip my hand around
the gun, and jump down off the fence.

"Get off him."

Sprowitz laughs.

When I pull the gun out, the tool falls from my pocket and skitters across the cement. Sprowitz doesn't see the gun because he's
distracted by the tool. "Where'd you get that?" He reaches out and
picks it up with one hand, still gripping Hafeez.

"I mean it. Let him go."

Sprowitz looks up and now he sees the gun. His face goes blank for a second. "Hey, no need for violence," he says.

"Let him go or I'll shoot you."

He shoves Hafeez forward. Hafeez staggers, struggling for air.

"Why are you here?" I say.

"I get my orders from your uncle. Really nice guy. He sure likes for you to be looked after."

"Jane told him where I was?"

"She's a great therapist, huh? She's really helped you out." He smirks.

"Have you been working with them all this time?"

"We go way back, Alicia. Don't you know that?"

I shake my head. "What? You just moved here."

He holds the tool up and twists it. "Where'd you get this again?"

"What does Alex want from me?"

"He just wants you on his side. It's simple. He doesn't want you to turn out like your father." Sprowitz says this so genuinely that it seems like he believes he's doing the right thing by me, like he honestly thinks he's on my side.

Hafeez is struggling to stand, still wheezing.

"Don't talk about my father," I say. "What does Alex really want?"

"He wants me to take you in."

"In where?"

Sprowitz puts the tool in his jacket pocket and takes a step toward me. "In," he says.

"Don't come any closer."

"In," he says again, taking another step.

"Don't do this, please," Hafeez says.

"In." Sprowitz keeps walking, until the muzzle of the gun is touching his chest. He grabs my hand and raises the gun so that it digs into the soft flesh under his chin. "Go ahead." He closes his eyes.

Does Sprowitz want me to kill him? I know what it is to feel that way. How bad is it to be him?

I can't kill Brian Sprowitz. I'm terrified, my body shocked by a surge of adrenaline. But I don't feel any ripping sensation inside of myself. There's no real decision here. I'm not a killer.

And then Sprowitz's eyes flash open. "Is this the world where you pull the trigger? Or is this the world where things go a different way?"

I try to yank the gun away from him, but he holds it close and so tightly that I know he senses the trembling in my hands. Our eyes are inches apart; we're locked together in a kind of awful embrace. He keeps the gun jammed into his neck, but his face softens. He looks almost hopeful. "Tell me," he says. "Which way does it go?"

"I don't know what you mean," I say.

Sprowitz closes his eyes like this pains him, and then I see it—that little kid in the picture of me at the birthday party, the one smiling so hard that I couldn't place him in my memory. It's a little Brian Sprowitz. I open my mouth to say something, but then something hardens in his expression, and I know this is going to get ugly.

"No!" Hafeez shouts because he knows it, too.

Then in one swift motion, Sprowitz twists the gun from my hand and cracks it against my head.

PART II
SPLIT

CHAPTER ELEVEN

THE ACHE comes first—a blunt pang in my skull—then lights, bright ones overhead. A bed with a white sheet, my own legs beneath it. Plastic cinch cuffs on my wrists, locked to shiny metal bedrails on either side.

A narrow, pale face blooms over me. "Alicia?" A woman's voice.

I squeeze my eyes shut for a second. White heat spreads through my head.

Jane—her face is blurry, as if we're both trapped underwater, a dark lake. I try to lift my head but the sharp pain sends me back down. I feel the tug of wires—small nodes taped on my temples and across my forehead, spiraling to a computer, where they all sync to one thick wire, and the deep throb of an IV in my right arm. The jagged line of my heartbeat blips across one monitor, and on another is a scan of what must be my brain.

"Where am I? What is all this?"

"It's for your own safety. You had a breakdown," Jane says.

My vision seems to fade in and out; I have to work hard to keep my focus. "Aren't you tired of lying to me yet?"

Jane ignores my question. "How are you feeling?"

I don't want her to cough up sympathy for me, especially since she knows more than she's let on. Wasn't she the one who told Sprowitz where I was? "You're in on it, aren't you? Whatever *this* is. Where's my father?"

"You won't find him," she says. "Even if you knew the location, you couldn't get to him, believe me."

"So Alex has him locked up, like me?"

Jane's face looks pale and flat, like a child's sidewalk chalk drawing. "Alicia, listen. Alex is going to come in here." She's so close to me I see her lips moving, but the sound is out of sync. "Don't tell him about the worlds, no details. Don't tell him about the one that's cracking. Don't tell him about the boy in that world. Okay? Promise me."

It's hard to follow her. Other worlds. The boy. I had talked to her about him in therapy after Sprowitz punched Hafeez. I picture Hafeez's shocked face in the alleyway where Sprowitz found us. "What happened to Hafeez?"

"He's safe at home now."

"I don't believe you." I see her through a halo, gaudy and shifting.

"You don't have to. Just do what I'm telling you. Please."

"What about my mother?"

"She's already been in to see you."

She's lying. My mother wouldn't leave me here. Or maybe she would, if Alex talked her into it.

"Let me talk to Hafeez. I want to know that he's okay. Then I'll promise not to say anything to Alex."

She glances at the door.

"Just one call," I say. "Even prisoners get that much."

She takes a deep breath and then reaches into her pocket and pulls out her phone. "You can't tell him where you are."

"I don't know where I am." It's the truth, and for a second I feel disconnected from everyone and everything. I could be *anywhere,* cast off like an astronaut somersaulting in slow motion away from the earth.

I tell her the number. I know it by heart. She punches it in and hits speaker. It rings once, twice, three times, and I'm sure that I'll have to leave a message. What the hell should I tell him?

But then he picks up. "Hello?" he says, his voice muffled.

"Hafeez," I say. "Are you okay?"

"Are *you* okay?"

Then I hear his mother's voice telling him to hang up.

He shouts, "Just give me a minute. I won't do drugs just by talking to her." He then says to me, "Sprowitz drugged me up, dropped me off, and told my parents you're the bad influence." I try to imagine Hafeez on drugs. He's not the type. "I'm not even supposed to be talking to you," he says. "But, God, it's great to hear your voice."

"Great to hear yours and I'm sorry I dragged—"

He cuts me off.

"Sprowitz took the tool."

"Yeah, but only here, right?" Exactly. Hafeez and I have it in the other world.

His mother's still shouting and closer to the phone now, so he starts talking fast. "I don't know if I'm going to be much help. Not *this* me, if you know what I mean. But maybe you can ask—" And then I know his mother's snatched the phone from him. The line goes dead.

I hand the phone to Jane, who puts it back in her pocket.

"You let Sprowitz drug Hafeez so he wouldn't be allowed to . . . what? Help me?"

"It was a compromise," Jane said. "At least he's not dead." I search her expression. She's serious. I'm scared suddenly in a way I wasn't before.

"This is much bigger than you can imagine," Jane whispers. "Did your father tell you where the atlas is?"

"What atlas? I don't know what you're talking about."

I can tell she doesn't believe me. "The one in our families for generations," she says flatly.

Our families? I don't say a word.

"Well, if he did tell you, don't say anything about that either."

She leans closer to me. "Alicia, there are so many things I never got to explain to you." Her voice is shaky and breathless. "I never answered your question about speaking Russian. You *can* speak other languages. When you enter a branch, the other consciousness is still there, aware of you, just subservient, and knowledge of life in that branch is a hum of information you can tap into." Jane pinches the bridge of her nose. "There are a million things I should have said about being a spandrel. I couldn't."

"Spandrel"—the word itself sounds like "spanning" and "tendril"—spanning worlds like tendrils. Like new green branches.

"Tell me now," I say.

Jane grips her hands together and keeps talking. "There are roots, too. Each decision has a thin shadow, an irrational what-if. It bubbles up from the subconscious. Those worlds in the roots aren't governed by the same laws of nature that we have."

I remember the fear that shot through me as I took the gun—a fear that I was insane and I'd never belong anywhere and that I'd be cut off from that moment on. Did that fear form a root?

"Roots are born from the subconscious the way dreams are." Jane is talking fast now. "But you don't have to worry about root worlds. You can't access your roots, not really; very few spandrels can." She pauses here, looks at the electrical nodes on my head. "Each of us has to develop our own way of entering the worlds we make."

Each of *us*. *Our*. "You're a spandrel, too?" I'm furious. My head's buzzing. "All those hours of talking! Why didn't you tell me?"

"Shhh," Jane says, her voice a harsh whisper. "Yes," she says, "but I'm not anymore. I got cut."

"Cut?"

She keeps her eyes glued to the computer screen. "I had that hyper-evolved part of my brain excised."

I ask Jane why she got cut. "Who would do that?"

"It's a hard way to live. You might know what I mean one day." Her face flushes; she looks like she's going to cry. "When Alex arrives, do what he says. I wish I could save you—from all of this, but I can't. I'm so sorry."

I reach for her but I'm still cuffed. "What happened to my father?"

She straightens, looks at the clock on the wall.

"Is my father dead?"

Her eyes are distant. She's scared. She whispers, "No. But . . ."

As her voice trails off, an older man wearing scrubs, mask and all, steps into the room. He's tall and angular with light brown skin and large worried eyes. "Everything okay?" he asks.

"Fine," Jane says, patting her pocket as if she's suddenly lost something.

"Alex wants you to keep her sedated." He pulls down his mask. He's a good bit older than Jane.

"Olsson," Jane whispers, "please."

Olsson. The one I overheard Jane talking to on the phone in her office.

He strides into the room. "We have no choice." He touches her shoulder gently, almost fatherly.

"But you do have a choice," I say. "You really do."

He looks at me, smiles—like he's happy to see me. I don't know why. He starts to say something to me, but Jane stops him. "I've already said too much."

He nods, takes a deep breath, and walks quickly out of the room.

"Jane, don't put me under," I tell her. "I need to think. I need my head. Please don't."

"I have to," she whispers. "You don't understand my role."

"Talk to me then. Explain it."

She takes a breath. She wants to confess, I can tell. But she stops herself and walks to the metal table, pulls out a box from a drawer. She lifts a needle.

"Don't. Please don't. Let's talk about this."

She inserts the needle into the tubing that leads to my IV. "Close your eyes," she says. "Right now, you can surrender a little."

"Jane," I plead, even though it's too late.

And then I'm suddenly desperately tired. I won't find my father. Something terrible has happened to him, I'm sure of it. I'm a spandrel—spandrel, spandrel, spandrel—but what does that really mean? I fight to keep my thoughts straight, but the room is already hazy at its edges.

I stare at her face, but it's as if the chalk-face I imagined earlier is being splattered by rain, washed away—splotch by splotch. She's cut. I wonder what that would be like. There's a Plath poem about a heart being stored in a box and not being able to know who you are. I try to remember it, to whisper it. My lips feel numb.

And then, Jane is at my bedside, and she leans in close to pull up the sheet, as if tucking me in like a little kid. She whispers, her voice low and ragged with urgency, "Your father told you to get Jax out of that branch. If you don't, he'll die there."

I think, *Won't they all?* and picture Jax's face, his blue eyes, his stare, but I can't hold it in place. The memory of his face blurs and then fades to pure light.

CHAPTER TWELVE

A HAND on my jaw.

A dark room.

One eye is forced open wide, drilled with light.

Blinding.

Then the other.

My uncle's face, blurred and doubling, leans over me.

My eyes sting and tear. I blink to clear my vision.

My wrists are still cuffed. The computer screen glows blue. My head aches, a deep unwavering pain.

The small windows are dark.

"Where's my father?" My throat is rough.

"I'll never understand it, Alicia. Your father's been gone all these years, and I'm the one who's been here all along."

I lift my arms, cuffed to the bedrails. "It's a relationship based on deep trust, right? Mutual respect? Honesty?" I hate my uncle for wasting years of my life, not telling me the truth—not preparing me. "I know what I am now. Why didn't you tell me?"

"I don't expect you to understand, but I really have wanted the best for you. And I couldn't tell you things before. I can now," he says, stuffing his hands into the pockets of his white lab coat.

"I want to know where Dad is. I want to see him."

"Your father's dangerous."

"He didn't seem dangerous to me."

"He's dangerous to the prime. To this world we call our own," Alex says. "Think about it. If you had access to all of these other worlds, wouldn't you take advantage of the opportunity?"

"I don't know what you're talking about."

"These branches," he says, "they're useful, *essential* really, to scientific advancement. During World War II, we tested the A-bomb in the desert of the prime, Alicia. No one has to do that anymore. We have worlds for that. Weapons, alternative fuels, global economic market shifts, responses to emergencies of all kinds. We can test these things out in the branches, and when we do, we strengthen the prime. We're saving lives."

I remember the TV footage of the nuclear bomb going off when the old man was stitching up my gunshot wound in that old hotel room, and then the drone I saw in one of those worlds, the people in hazmat suits, the quarantine camp in the world where Jax is, where my mother is dying. "You think the people in those worlds are lab rats?"

"Do you want us to play out the apocalypse in the prime? Right now, for example, there's a branch in which a vaccination called RO Two was tested on a virus. Heard of it?"

I shake my head no.

"The virus was developed in a test tube. Biological warfare. It only exists in two locations in this world. Well, as far as we know. And no one has any defense against it. If it fell into the wrong hands here, it would decimate the world's population in three to four years. So we tested the RO Two vaccine in a branch world. It didn't work.

The company has developed another vaccine, and we'll test it in another branch until we get it right. And the branches aren't going to survive if the prime doesn't. They depend on the prime as their main source. If we're not healthy, they're not healthy."

"And what does my father have to do with this?"

"Some people can't see the value in what we're doing. Progress always finds resistance, and, yes, your father plays a large role among them. They're just a bunch of thugs and petty mobsters, really." Alex stands up, paces. "I've had people hunting him down. My own brother. You can't know how that feels. But I had to, and I've got him nailed in every world he has access to. Do you know why he came to your birthday party after all these years?"

"Tell me."

"It's hard to say this." Alex runs his hand over his closely cropped hair and sighs. "But he showed up because you're finally of some use to him." He picks up a folder sitting on the computer's keyboard, opens it, and picks up a stack of photographs. "Your father knows you're about to get some power and he needs you to get something for him. You think he's been holding on to these pictures out of nostalgia? He was hoping to show them to you, offer you a little proof of how much you've bonded in every world except this one. But he's been playing you, Alicia. What do you really know about him? What are your actual memories of him as a dad?"

Would my father just use me? My head is ringing. I push it back into the pillow. I suddenly see all of my father's worlds in a twisted way. What kind of father lets his daughter run around in a sinking cruise ship while being hunted down by men with guns? What kind of a father leaves his daughter with her grandfather in a world boiling with chemical fires or where the television loops an image of a mushrooming nuclear bomb?

And what kind of father abandons his daughter when she's just a toddler? Abandons her and doesn't come back for a dozen years, and then only when he needs her? All my old fear and anger surfaces quickly, like it's been waiting for my father to disappoint, to prove he's unreliable, never loved me, and is just going to abandon me all over again. "No," I say. "He's not using me. That's not true." I can't give up on him, because it means giving up on some part of myself.

Alex puts the pictures in the pocket of his lab coat. "He didn't mention something that's important to him? A certain kind of book that's been in our family for generations? My father was supposed to give that book to me, Alicia. Did he tell you what's in it?"

I don't say anything. I don't want Alex to know what I've been told.

"All of the old spandrel families, all of their access points, all of their triggers. The atlas unlocks worlds, Alicia. The possibilities are endless."

"Use your own damn worlds for your experiments!"

"I can't."

"Why not?"

"It's genetic. If your father has blue eyes, maybe you won't, but maybe your brother will."

"You're not a spandrel."

He shakes his head.

"So you just sell off spandrels' worlds? I guess it would be nice for you to have the atlas, too? Not just my father."

"That doesn't matter to me as much as you do," Alex says.

I lean forward, held back by the restraints. "Bullshit! If you care so much about me, why do you have me locked up here? And"—I think of Sprowitz pushing the gun under his own jaw—"you sent Sprowitz to drag me in. He works for you. Did you set Sprowitz up across the street from me, too?"

Alex nods calmly. "Sprowitz was supposed to keep an eye on you. Maybe help create a situation where you'd have to make a real choice. Have you branched already?"

I keep quiet.

"You did."

I don't respond, and Alex presses his thin lips together and shakes his head. He turns toward the darkened window. I can see his reflection in the glass, his face shadowed with anger. "Stubborn, like your father." He sighs, pacing. "If you really are like him, Alicia, then you might not even just be an ordinary spandrel. You might be one of the rare ones, and it's one of the rare ones that we might need."

"What do you mean?"

"Some rarities can move a physical object between branches. They can piggyback things, sometimes even people. A spandrel with the power to piggyback can even bring a nonspandrel into another world."

"So my father could piggyback you into another world if he wanted."

"I never asked him to. I believe in loyalty—to people and to your world. Your father took off when he was around your age. When I was twenty, he showed up again. He was already leading multiple lives, jumping from one branch to another. When one life got too hard, he'd leave—dodging responsibility, taking the easy route, hopping from world to world. I wish he'd never found us again. But I've stayed. I've been loyal."

Should I wish that my father never showed up in the backyard with the birthday present? Maybe it wasn't much of a present after all. Maybe he gave it to me only to help me do what he wants me to do.

"Tell me what it feels like, moving between your father's worlds." Alex reaches into his pocket and pulls out the small flashlight he used to check my eyes. He points it at the floor and clicks it on and off and on again. "Is it like running away?"

I think about how I would sometimes lean into those worlds, hoping to disappear. But it's not like running away. If anything, it's like running toward.

"Your father was good at running away," Alex says. "I wouldn't have done that to you. I never would."

I can't help but defend my father. "Maybe he didn't do that to me, either." The birthday pool party, the bulldog puppy, the butterfly beating its wings while clinging to a stick—those were real, weren't they?

Alex turns and walks toward me. "You know there's one world that he's dead in, Alicia. I've heard spandrels can sense the deadness of a world's creator. Isn't there a world where you just don't feel him anymore?"

I refuse to answer, but he's right. Jax's world. I've never sensed my father in it.

"He lives a dangerous life and it caught up with him there."

I don't know whether or not to mourn a version of my father that I never knew existed. I feel the grief anyway—even though I don't understand it. I want my head to stop hurting. I want my uncle to stop talking. I want to close my eyes and start over. But I can't. The questions are in my head. "Are all of my father's worlds doomed?"

"Worlds are like any living organism. Survival of the fittest applies to them as well. If enough people die, there aren't enough to perceive the world. If there aren't enough to perceive the world, it's no longer fixed. It begins to crumble."

I think of Jax's world, of the tree—half alive and half dead. Jax said it was an experiment, that the people only gave their attention to half the tree, the living half. Maybe enough people have died in that world to start the decaying process. That means the survivors—

the few of them left, including one version of me, my dying mother, Alex, and Jax—will die with it.

"But I exist in those worlds. . . ." I whisper. I feel like my chest is too full of blood. It's pumping too hard.

"You have to get on my side, Alicia. I can take care of you in a way your father can't. Even when I made mistakes, I was always trying to do right by you and your mother. I was trying to protect you. What has your father ever done for you?"

I stare at the ceiling. And then I see the picture in my head of my father and me as a toddler. The snowman. The flakes swirling around us. The picture I've looked at all my life.

"Once," I whisper, "he made a snowman with me."

Alex runs his knuckles slowly down the side of his face. "Is that what you're going with? One flimsy memory?"

"That's all I need," I say, and it's true. All I have are tiny bits and pieces of a man. Maybe it's all anyone ever has—just pieces of a person. "I'll always choose my father. Every time."

Alex's cheeks stiffen. He swallows hard. He seems to swell with anger. He looks different suddenly, taller, more angular. His eyes flood with tears, but they stay locked there, shining. "You want to see your father? Is that what you want?" He walks to the computer and taps a few keys.

An image appears on the screen from what seems to be a sur-veillance camera. My father is strung up by his wrists. He's been beaten. Shirtless, his body twists by the cords bound to a ceiling not in frame; I see his chest, his arms, part of his back—blood smeared over his black tattoos—branches curling in all directions, up his arms, and snaking down his back. His head is bent. His swol-len face looks dead.

"Is he alive?" My voice is barely a whisper, and then I scream, "Is he alive?"

"We're trying to save him," Alex says. "If he would just give up, we wouldn't have to . . ."

My father lifts his head as if he can hear us. And in that moment he doesn't look weak to me. He has refused to give in. Whatever he's holding on to, he's willing to die for it.

His eyes fix on an image—a screen? Can he see me? "Alicia," he says, his voice barely there.

"Yes," I say, looking into the computer's embedded camera. "It's me."

His eyes squint and well up.

I want him to know I've branched, that things have changed the way he said they would, but I don't want Alex to know. I say, "I remember."

The edges of his lips curl up slightly. He knows what I mean: pieces of our lives together in other worlds, my childhoods, are coming back to me.

"I'm sorry," I choke out, my voice strangled by emotion. "I didn't get lost and stay lost."

He shakes his head. "Don't." Don't apologize or don't hide?

"Ask him about the atlas," Alex whispers to me.

"He doesn't know where it is."

"I think we have a win-win, here," Alex says to us, and his voice sounds different. It sounds real and honest, it has an edge, as if all of his concern and worry for me has been peeled off. Gone. And what's left is a broken man—sick and twisted—but real. "Let's give her a couple days to find the atlas, or we kill you, Ellington. Meanwhile, you can save her by telling us where it is at any time."

"Don't do this to her," my father says. "Don't."

"I'll do what's best for Alicia," Alex says. "And she belongs where she belongs."

My father lets out a guttural scream. His hands look like bloodless claws over his head. And then, with what seems like the last burst of his strength, he pushes his legs back and then up and over his head, kicking the camera so that it jerks away from him.

There's a crash, the camera toppling, and now all I see is a hotel room—a bed pushed against a wall, a broken lamp, blood spattered on the walls and a set of curtains, light slicing through a one-foot break in them, the small view of circular window panes. Someone jerks the camera and my father is back in frame.

My father stops fighting the ropes. His body sways. He says, "Alex, leave her alone. Let her go. I don't know where the atlas is, Alex. I don't. Let me go and I'll track it down; please, listen—"

Alex hits a key and the screen goes dark.

I can't take my eyes off it. "You heard him. He doesn't know where the atlas is," I say. "He'd have told you already. If my mother knew what you were doing . . ."

At the mention of my mother, all his old soft tones come rushing back into his voice. "But she won't know," he says. "She's already been to see you. She saw you were in good hands. After all, you ran away and took a gun with you. I'm sure you can understand that she would prefer to keep you contained for a while. Who would believe you, Alicia? Troubled in school, on all kinds of meds, therapy—it's not likely you'd get far trying to report any of this to anyone."

I close my eyes. My chest aches for all the trouble I've caused my mother. But I have to convince Alex to let my father go.

"This atlas. What if he's the only one who can find it? If you've got him locked up like that, he never will. Don't you see that?"

"I have people depending on me. There's so much opportunity out there, things we can do that will help the prime."

"Like unleashing global epidemics? I think the universe could use a little less of your help."

He stares at me for a moment as if he's adding something up in his head. "Can you still see your other self in the branch you created? Typically spandrels can."

I look back at him, silent.

"You know, that other Alicia is just as real as you are. It would be too bad if something happened to her."

I take a deep breath. It's true that the responsibility I feel for her, and for that world, is huge. My chest hurts thinking of her, my mother, Hafeez in that world, vulnerable.

"I can't help you," I say. "I don't even know where to start looking."

"Well, I'm sorry to hear that. So you'll stay locked up here where you can't run. And your father might hang in there another day or two. Or maybe you'll decide to help him out."

My head is pounding again, my heart racing at the thought of being trapped here indefinitely. And letting my father suffer. "Those pictures," I say, "they're mine. You can't take them." I want to hold on to the truth.

Alex shakes his head as if he's really tired and then walks to the door, pauses, and, without looking back, he says, "You know, I introduced your parents, way back when."

My voice comes out shaky. "You did?"

He nods. "I'd regret that too, but then there's you. You're the upside of all that, Alicia. Where would I be without you now?" He flashes a smile, a sad one, and leaves.

CHAPTER THIRTEEN

I NEED to find Jax. His mother knew where the atlas was. Before my father knew she was dead, he wanted me to tell her that if the world was about to die, she needed to get the atlas out and that he wouldn't be able to help. Maybe she told Jax where the atlas was before she died. No matter what, it's the only lead I have.

And I've got to have blood. My wrist is cuffed to the bed railing, and, where the railing can be raised and lowered, there's a sharp metal lip. It's hard to make myself do it, but I scrape my skin against it, managing to open a small cut just under the heel of my hand.

I concentrate on the blood. I hope it gets me where I need to be. Then something shifts, my body pulses with pain. I wedge my shoulder under the bedrails and push my collarbone against the metal. The pain zeros in.

I see red, widening, widening. . . .

———

. . . I'm kneeling on pavement, picking up pill bottles as fast as I can and shoving them into a canvas bag. I'm near a loading dock, behind what seems to be a strip mall.

"Hurry up!" It's a guy a little older than I am, lean, unshaven. He's gathering pill bottles, too.

And then a beam from a flashlight pops up.

"Run!" the guy shouts.

We take off down the length of the strip mall. The man with the flashlight starts running after us, big heavy strides.

We run into a thin strip of woods. The ground is rutted and pocked. A pair of headlights shines on the other side, a pickup truck waiting for us.

The guy running with me reaches the truck first and tosses the bag to the driver and tells me to get in.

"What about you?" I ask him.

"I've got more to do out here."

The driver leans toward the open door. "So, Pynch, how'd she do?" It's Jax, wearing what might have been a dress shirt, but it's worn thin, cuffed up above his elbows. He's smiling a little, and I haven't really seen his smile before.

"Pretty good for a rookie," Pynch says, and then he claps my back.

I slide into the passenger's seat. Pynch slams the door, taps the hood, and gives a wave before darting back into the woods.

Jax shoves the truck in reverse then pulls the wheel hard and drives off across a stubbled field. "Glad you guys are okay." His face is lit by the dashboard, the profile of his jaw and lips, the glint of his eyes.

"I'm not me," I say quickly.

"I didn't think so," he says, glancing at me. "There was something about—I don't know—your expression, your eyes. I've been waiting for you to come back."

"So you know what's going on?" I say. "You know about spandrels?"

"My mother told me everything before she died," Jax says. He bumps the truck up onto a narrow country road.

"Have you—"

"Branched? No, but I know it's coming." His eyes look a little glassy. "This place forces you to make hard decisions."

It feels so strange to talk to someone who gets it. I want to ask a million questions, but there's no time. "Did your mother tell you about an atlas?"

He nods. "It's hidden in a different world. She told me your father knows the trigger to get into that world."

"I can't exactly talk to my father right now to find that out."

"I'm talking about your father in this world."

"Alex?"

"No, your real father. He knows the world, its trigger. He just doesn't know that he knows."

How does he know Alex isn't my real father? Did his mother tell him? "My real father's dead in this world, isn't he?"

He mutters, "One way of putting it."

"What does *that* mean?"

"Listen, Alicia, here's the thing: I don't know what world the atlas is hidden in or how to access it, but my mother told me where to look once inside of that world."

My hand starts buzzing. I try to fight it off.

"I'm supposed to get you out of here," I tell him quickly. "My father wanted me to—and—"

"This is my world," Jax says. "I don't exist in the prime."

"How is that possible?"

Jax pulls over. Through the open windows, I hear the groan and squeak of the nearby dying trees. He smiles. "You don't know the whole story then, do you?"

"What story?" My lower ribs on one side start to ache. I try to ignore it, but I know I'm wincing with pain. "Tell me."

"Look, it's not your problem," Jax says. "Your family's done enough."

Through the open window, I hear a tree fall—loud and heavy—and then another creaks like an old ship and it gives in, too.

I lean over trying to endure the pain in my ribs, willing it away. "Where's it hurt?"

"My lower-back ribs. God, I wish I could make it stop."

"You don't know how to stay in a world? How would you know how to piggyback someone from branch to branch?"

I shrug, a little breathless.

He reaches around my waist on both sides. I feel the electricity of his touch. "Give me your hand. Show me where it's the most painful."

His hand on top of mine, warm and dry, I point out the spot on my back, my lower ribs on my left side. "Here."

"Okay then," he says. He takes my hand in both of his. "To stop yourself from leaving a world, you have to find the pressure point on the opposite side of your body." He moves my hand to my right side, the lowest rung of my ribs, and with my hand under his, he pushes. I feel my cheeks blush. The ache eases in my left side.

"That's amazing!"

"Simple," he says.

"Look, if I can figure out which world to go to, will you help me get the atlas out? You're the only person who can help me and—"

"Without knowing how to get into that world, I can't help you.

And I don't want to be rescued. I want this world to be saved. And it can't be saved. So you can't help me."

"I guess not." My ribs are buzzing again, and this time I let them. Why am I here? Why am I even trying? It's all a lost cause. Wind kicks up some dust, and each individual speck catches in the head-lights.

"What went wrong in this place?" I hear myself say.

"Don't you know? The virus. There's no cure." I hear Jax's voice through a haze of lit motes pulling and blurring. And I realize this might be the world Alex sold off for testing the RO2 vaccine.

"Wait!" I say.

"Alicia, go. There's no helping us. Not here."

He reaches around my waist again to my lower ribs, this time to the ones that ache. I don't want to fade out of this world, especially not now, my eyes locked with his, the sound of the dying world wheezing and falling around us. "I have to be here. I'll go down with this ship. You do what you can to save yourself."

His face blurs as if he's underwater, being pulled away from me on some invisible current. . . . I reach for him and keep reaching, but then I'm the one who's gone. . . .

. . . Rumbling. Vibrations.

Hafeez is driving his mom's ancient Volvo with its crappy muf-fler. We're a few blocks from my house, driving away from it. It's dark. "So which book do you like more," Hafeez says, "*The Hidden Reality* or *The Elegant Universe*? Brian Greene is pretty good, right? I mean, he breaks it all down. He writes for the masses, but it's solid."

"Yeah," I say, "Brian Greene." I have no idea what we're talk-ing about. I pull down the visor and look at my chin in the vanity mirror. Stitches. I run my fingers over them. I'm in the world where

I didn't take the gun. My first branch. I don't want to announce myself to Hafeez because I know he'll freak, and it was weird between us last time, but I know I have to soon.

I look behind us, wondering if we're being followed. There's another car. I memorize it.

"You get Schrödinger's cat, right?"

"Kind of."

"It's just that the cat in the box can be either alive or dead but only until you open the lid and perceive its life or death form. It's all about perception."

"I see." I don't see. Hafeez turns and the car behind us does, too.

"Deepak says that perceptions create reality. You gotta love Chopra." He smiles, flips on a blinker, takes a turn.

Perceptions create reality. The half-dead tree, the half-living tree. Jax's world is dying because of a lack of perception. "Gotta."

"I also came across this thing called a biocentric universe. Life creates the universe, not the other way around. We're not alone, Alicia. The universe isn't here for us or despite us, but because of us."

I glance back again. Same headlights.

"I think someone is tailing us," I say.

"*Tailing* us? Who says 'tailing' anymore?"

"Where are we going exactly?"

Hafeez whips around and looks at me. "Breaking and entering," he says. "Jane's office. Your idea. But it's not you, is it?"

"It's me—the other me, and I think we're going to need to lose the car behind us. Get on I-93. The exit is coming up."

He dutifully turns on his blinker.

"What the hell, Hafeez? You don't use a blinker in a high-speed chase!"

"Has the high-speed chase started? Did you make an announcement? Because, if so, I missed it." He gets into the right lane but seems to be hesitating.

"I don't have time for your prissy driver's-ed shit, Hafeez! Turn now!" I reach for the wheel.

"Okay! Shit!" He swerves onto the ramp. The bluish tint of the silver car's headlights are still close behind.

"There's a place with no barriers up ahead, right? Where they're doing construction and there's a gap."

"My mother will kill me if I ding this car!"

"This car? Didn't she buy it pre-dinged?"

"Owning a Volvo was very important for my mother—asserting the American dream and all."

"Volvos are Swedish!"

He has both hands tight on the wheel and has started to gun it a little, including some polite weaving through traffic. "Don't mess with an American dream!"

I glance back over my shoulder. "Look, we're in real trouble. This isn't our old Sprowitz-in-a-lunch-line level of shit. This is men-with-guns, torturers, killers. That level."

"Okay," he says, and then adds a panicked, "Shit, shit, shit."

I take a deep breath. "You can do this." I speak as soothingly as I can. "I want you to drive through the gap, okay?"

The headlights are closer on us now.

"You're going to slow down, not with the brake, just let off the gas, and then whip through." He nods but I'm not sure he's actually listening. "It's coming now. No brakes, okay?"

"Screw you—you don't even have a license," he says angrily.

Now I know he can do it. Pissed is better than scared. "Here it comes."

The headlights are on our bumper. I make out the gap ahead. "See it?"

He nods, whispers, "I don't want to be a dead cat in Schrödinger's box. I don't want to be a dead cat in Schrödinger's box," and then he swerves. I brace.

He slides through, except the Volvo's fender scrapes the barrier on the turn and the car fishtails. But he rights it quickly, pulling the wheel hard, and I see the silver car pass by. I hear the squeal of brakes and horns blaring.

"God damn it!" Hafeez shouts happily. "I'm good! Did you see that?"

"Get off at the next exit."

"I can't wait to tell you about it—the other you. I knew it wasn't you. You just weren't being the girl who kissed me."

I remembered the kiss when I was in that world. It was a shadow of a memory, like a story told to you in a dream. But I don't want Hafeez to know I remember. It might freak him out, so I play dumb. "I kissed you?"

"You didn't, but the other you. But, yes, you did. Or I kissed you. Or something like that."

"Really?"

"Is that so hard to believe?"

"No, but . . ."

"You're different, you know. The other you."

"How?"

"Hard to explain." And then he smiles. He tries to rein it in, but that only makes his smile even brighter.

"What is it?"

"You're great," he says softly.

"The other me?"

"I'm kind of . . ."

"You're kind of what?"

"I hope it's okay, but . . ." He pounds the wheel a few times with the heel of his hand. "I'm kind of crazy about the other you!"

I'm not sure what to say. He's not telling me that he likes *me*, but I still blush. "Good," I say. "I'm happy for you." And the other me too. I mean, maybe I've wondered if one day Hafeez and I could turn into something else. But I never wanted it, because if we broke up, we wouldn't get to be friends anymore. But now it's happened and there's no turning back.

"You said kissing me made you feel like your heart was some flower, blooming, but in distress. Plath, right?"

"I said that? Me?"

"You whispered it. I don't even know if I was supposed to hear it."

"A red-bell," I tell him now. "It's in one of her poems—'a red bell-bloom,' yes."

"That kind of got me." He curls his fist lightly and knocks on his heart, three little taps, like it's a secret sign between the two of them. Then he smiles, suddenly shy. "You sure it's okay? It's weird, I know, but—"

"But good," I say. And then I feel incredibly lonely. Some other version of myself falls for someone without me, almost immediately. And what about me? But then I imagine the two of them together. I can see them in Hafeez's garage. They're both leaning against the Volvo's passenger door in the dark, holding hands, staring at each other, laughing a little, talking. She kisses him. He kisses her back. I feel like I shouldn't be able to see this. It's not my memory, not my world, but I do, for just a second, and then it's gone. They're right for each other. Not Hafeez and me, but Hafeez and her. I'm someone else. It's getting clearer and clearer to me. Like that crack in the frozen lake has splintered in all directions, with one deep crack that divides it completely. I'm someone who set out, who took a risk. This is who I am and I just keep taking more risks.

I feel my right hand buzz and, like Jax taught me, I just squeeze the spot on my left.

"So what happened in the other branch?" Hafeez asks.

I try to bring him up to speed as quickly as I can, but when I get to Alex and my father strung up in a hotel room, I stop short. "I just need the atlas. That's all."

It dawns on me I haven't asked why we're headed to Jane's office. We can't really be looking for the atlas here. I'm sure she doesn't know where it is. "What are we looking for at Jane's?"

"We've been combing your memories," Hafeez says. "You tell me as many details as possible, looking for any kinds of clues we can find."

I know that this is how the other Alicia and Hafeez got closer. It was all the confiding, the way Hafeez listens. That's what makes him different from other people. That Alicia existed more when she was with him—him seeing her for who she really was. Maybe if perception really does create reality, then it was his perception of her—really paying attention—that made her feel more alive.

"And when we went over the moment that Jane asked you to tell her about the boy in the other world, you remembered she'd opened her desk drawer. She was looking at something."

"So that's what we're going to try to find? That one thing?"

"We don't have much, Alicia. We have to do everything we can with anything we have."

I nod. He's right.

I give him a few more directions, and now we're so close my stomach flips.

"Nice neighborhood," Hafeez says. Two gray-haired women are

power walking in puffy ankle-length coats down a sidewalk, lit only by streetlamps. "Where the hell am I?"

"Turn right here," I say. "Take the next left. Her house is the second on the right."

Hafeez shakes his head, still smiling, and lifts his hand. "Still shaking! My mom's going to shit about the bumper."

"Her American dream has a dent."

"Worth it. Worth every second! What's an undented American dream anyway? Huh?"

"Slow down," I say. "It's right up here."

Jane's upstairs lights are on. Her office is dark. "Pull around the corner."

He turns the wheel and then, two houses up, kills the engine. Without the noisy muffler, it's suddenly very quiet.

I grab the door handle, feeling jittery. "If I'm gone more than fifteen minutes, you should just leave."

"Ah, no." He shakes his head. "I'm coming with you."

"No you're not."

"Yes, I am. I don't want to be some stupid accomplice. I want in. Seriously. You owe me—for the shit I'm going to catch."

"You'll catch more shit if you're caught breaking and entering."

"I'm well aware of the risks."

We glare at each other. He doesn't blink.

"Fine," I say.

We get out of the car, walk past Jane's tall hedges and into the darkened side yard, where a narrow stone path leads to her office door.

"The room gets stuffy sometimes," I whisper. "There's one window that she cracks open during sessions when it's warmer outside. There's a chance she never locked it."

The yard is mostly blocked by trees. I nudge the window and it doesn't budge.

"Let me try," Hafeez whispers. He pushes hard. Nothing.

"Okay then."

"Okay then what?" he says.

I cover my hand with the sleeve of my jacket, a little afraid of my own confidence, and punch in the window. It's harder to do than I thought, but, muffled by my jacket, not too loud. A few shards fall to the floor, which is carpeted. "Okay then that," I say.

We wait to hear if the noise alerted Jane, but the house is quiet.

I slide my hand in, unlock the latch on the inside, and push the window open.

"That was kind of badass," Hafeez admits. "I'm seeing a whole new side of you."

"A whole new me, even." Hafeez laughs and I shush him.

I climb in, the cold air following me into the warm room. Hafeez then hoists himself up over the sill. I keep the pressure up on my left hand, a steady hold. I feel like I shouldn't be here. I'm invading her privacy, but then again, nothing I ever said in this room—where I thought I was safe—was ever kept private. She betrayed me.

Hafeez heads to her filing cabinet while I move quickly to her desk and pull open the thin drawer. Pens roll forward.

I see a faded picture. This is what she was looking at. A photograph of blanched dirt, big blue sky with an old oil pump tilted toward the earth.

And in the foreground, two people.

A little boy.

But not just any boy.

He's only eight or so, but I'd recognize him anywhere. In a flash, I know exactly where his hand last touched mine, his face lit by the pickup truck's dashboard.

Jax.

Here he is, standing next to a woman who is tan and lean and smiling.

A happy version of Jane Larkin.

I'm frozen.

"What is it?" Hafeez asks.

"Jax," I whisper, and maybe because I'm staring at his face, I feel a sharp shooting pain in my collarbone. His world is calling me to it. I grab the bone on the other side, push hard.

Hafeez has opened a drawer to Jane's filing cabinet and he's holding a file. "They're all blank files with blank pages," he says. "She's not a therapist at all."

Overhead, a cell phone chirps.

A muffled voice.

A loud bump.

I tuck the picture into my jacket pocket. "Let's go."

As Hafeez drives out of Jane's neighborhood, he doesn't say a word. I stare at the photograph. "When I told Jane about my first hallucination of Jax, she sat forward on her seat," I explain to Hafeez. "Now I know why. She knows about him, about that world. How? What do they mean to each other? There's a faint resemblance—the coloring, the nose. Do you think Jane is Jax's mother?"

"Anything's possible."

I put the picture back in my jacket pocket and look in the mirror to see if any cars are following us. It seems clear.

"I've got to go over some stuff with you," Hafeez says. "I need to talk to you while you're still you."

"What is it?"

"Open the glove compartment."

I turn the knob. "What am I looking for?"

"My stash of Pixy Stix. I do my best thinking with blue."

"So *that's* the secret." I pull out a blue Pixy Stix and hand it to him.

He pulls out his phone, hands it to me, and tells me how to pull up a certain screen—a scan of the photo of my dad and me, as a little kid, in the snow together.

"I put it under magnifying glass, just for kicks. Flip to the next image."

I swipe the screen, a close-up.

"Notice the inch of bare skin, exposed by the gap between his glove and jacket sleeve?"

There's the smallest dark tendril of ink from my father's tattoo. "I've seen parts of it in all of the worlds I've seen him in," I tell Hafeez, remembering my father's body strung up in that hotel room—that tattoo spanning his chest and back and arms.

"The way the other you explained the feelings you have just before you disappear and how a certain pain will flare up before you head into a certain world, plus the poem and the tattoos, we decided to look into acupressure. We went to this place called Yang's."

"Yang's?"

"It's a Chinese market where people buy squid ink and whatever. The old man in the back—the owner's grandfather or something—talked to us about acupressure, the mind-body connections. Go to the next screen."

I swipe again, and there's a human form, broken into a chart with different spots on the body labeled with combinations of letters and numbers.

"Acupressure points. I thought that the tattoo might follow all these points. Swipe again."

The next picture is one I recognize, Leonardo da Vinci's drawing of a man with outstretched arms and legs in a circle with a hand-drawn three over his chest and arms, following the dots that mark pressure points.

"Nice work," I say.

"Thanks," Hafeez says. "It's that art elective, and you helped some—the other you." It's still strange to hear about things I've done with only a dim echo of memory. "We showed him the gift your dad gave you, the tool." He reaches over and pops open the glove compartment. He pulls out bulky manila envelope and hands it to me. I open it to find the tool. "He told us it's used in reflexology, which mainly focuses on the hands and feet, but your father must use it all over his body."

I hold it in my right hand, and it feels exactly right again, like I'm meant to hold it. "To move faster between worlds."

"Right. You told me that there was this sensation, a really specific spot, that you felt like if you could just get at it, you'd be able to fade out faster."

"So, his tattoos aren't just tattoos," I say.

"They're a map of universes. His universes," Hafeez says, throwing back some more Pixy Stix.

"To move from one world to the next, I have to know both the trigger in my mind for that world and a trigger—a pressure point—inside of my own body, somewhere."

"And to get back again?"

"It's usually just in my hand. That's where I feel it. It's the whole mind-body connection, I think."

"Acupressure talks a lot about mind-body connections. Ancient medicine."

We find ourselves back in my neighborhood, with its pinched houses and rusted chain-link fences. Hafeez turns onto my street. The stupid plastic reindeer is still knocked over in the neighbor's yard. I've changed so much, but nothing else has changed at all. When we pull up to my house, my mother's car is in the drive, but the house is dark. "My mom," I say.

"What about her?"

"I have to ask her about the atlas. You never know . . ." I glance up at my house. "Thanks, Hafeez. For everything."

"No problem. Do me a favor. Write a note on your hand telling the other you to call me," he says. "When she gets in."

"Right. I will. Take care of her for me, okay?" I say.

Hafeez smiles. "I will."

I start to put the tool back in the glove compartment, but he stops me. "What are you doing? It's yours. Use it."

"Thanks."

I run up to the front door, unlock it, then turn back to Hafeez. He gives a wave, and I wave back.

As he drives off, I glance at Brian Sprowitz's bedroom window. He's not there.

I step inside, locking the door fast behind me.

CHAPTER FOURTEEN

A LIGHT is on in the kitchen but I only hear a strange clicking noise.

I follow the sound, walking through the living and the dining rooms. And then I see my mother, tapping on the dark glass of the sliding door with her nails, staring out at nothing.

"Mom?"

She turns with a small gasp. "You scared me."

I look out at the backyard, crusted with patches of snow. It's where my father showed up. Is some part of her hoping to find him there again?

"Are you okay?" I ask, gripping my left hand with my right.

"Of course," she says, and then she changes gears. "Where were you?"

"I was out with Hafeez." I put my hands in my jacket pockets. In one, I feel the tool and I'm happy to have it, relieved, actually.

"Good." Does she know the other me is dating him?

I have to bring up my father and the atlas—but I don't know how. My mother's taught me not to talk about him.

"I'm sorry I got mad at you about Dad."

She seems to shudder a bit at my mention of him. "What? No, it was nothing."

"It was strange to have him here," I say, trying to sound casual. "I've never asked you much about him, you know?"

"You used to and you stopped. Maybe you were being nice to me." She walks into the kitchen. She doesn't want to talk about my father now either. I feel an ache in my hand that could send me back to the prime. Part of me wants to run away from the conversation. Is that the lure my father felt? The ability to bail at any turn? Was Alex telling the truth about him—or one truth from many? I pinch my other hand and say, "Let me ask something."

She starts filling the sink with hot water, slips a dirty pot under the faucet. I'm about to ask her if my dad ever mentioned an atlas, and hiding it, but for some reason I stop and ask what I've never had the courage to before: "Why did you and Dad break up?"

She pours in a stream of liquid dish soap. "I wasn't enough. We weren't enough, I guess." Her voice cracks a little. The bubbles start expanding.

I don't know if I believe her. I have those photos—and memories—from other worlds that prove my father tried to hold on to me. "Or was there something about him you couldn't accept?"

"He's good deep down," she says, starting in with her old familiar lines.

"I don't want to hear that stuff. I want the truth."

She turns off the faucet and looks at me—the way you would a stranger. Am I a stranger? She takes in the way I'm applying pressure to my hand by pinching it, and she knows. I can see it in her eyes. She walks over to me and touches my cheek. "It's not been you, has it? I knew it." She lets her hand fall. "You're already gone."

"You know about spandrels, then. You've known all along." I'm furious suddenly. "What do you know? Tell me about my father, about moving between branches."

She slams her fists into her thighs and her eyes tear up. "We were so close. Alex said you were almost ready."

"Wait. Was I going to get cut? Was *that* the plan? The cure?"

She seems shocked that I know this. "I want you to have your life to live—your own life! Is that so bad?"

I shake my head. "There is no cure! Cutting isn't a cure! Alex wouldn't have done it anyway. He wanted me to be a spandrel, one who worked for him."

"You don't even know what that means." She walks back to the sink and reaches into the steaming water.

I think about telling her that some version of myself is cuffed to a bed under my uncle's watch and that he's trying to beat information out of my father, but I stop myself.

"You can be mad at me for trying to save you from it if you want to," she says, "but I'll never regret it."

"But this is who I am. Who I was meant to be."

"No," she says. "It's no life! They'll draw you in, and you won't be able to get out."

"Who will draw me in?"

She raises one hand, wet and slightly trembling, and eyes me searchingly. She turns back to the pots, scrubbing them. "You want to know how it all happened? I'll tell you. I was only eighteen, kicked out of foster care, no prospects, no family, nothing. And then this college boy fell for me. Alex. He'd had a rough childhood, too, but he had a way out. And we dreamed of getting out together. I'd never been in love. I didn't know anything about it."

I have trouble taking it all in. I'm not convinced my mother ever figured out anything about love.

She looks at the wall, her eyes quivering with tears but her expression stony. "So when Alex asked me to marry him, I said yes. I was being smart for once, I thought."

The picture over the mantel in the world that's cracking—did she marry him in that world? But then why did I look like me—part of my mother, part of my own father? I can't wrap my head around it.

My mother goes quiet for a moment, and when she starts to talk again, her voice is softer, sadder. "But then your father showed up, and we fell in love. Real love. The first time in my life." She glides her wet soapy hand along the counter. "And I got pregnant with you."

She looks at me and then out the dark window to the backyard. "Alex was furious. The way he sees it, your father stole me away from him. And he never got over it. He said I was all he ever wanted."

I lean on the doorjamb. My father stole my mother from Alex. It makes much more sense now—the way Alex talks about my mother like he knows her more than he has a right to. It's why he said he introduced them.

She puts the pots on a towel to dry. "Your father took me with him to another branch once. I couldn't live the way he needed to, on the run, jumping." Her voice trails off for a moment. She crosses her arms as if she's remembering cold winters. "When we got back, we fell apart. I had this feeling that our lives were fractured. I felt it inside of him and myself." She grips the front of her blouse with her still-damp hands. "I begged your father to get it cut out, to be free of it. It was the only way. That's what he refused to do—for us."

"You gave him an ultimatum," I say, "to either give up who he is or lose us. Is that it?"

"Yes. So that we could have a shot."

"A shot at what?"

"Living normal lives—here, together."

The answer this time is different, but it means the same thing, really. Healthy, to my mother, means normal. I feel like I can't breathe. "Is that the ultimatum you were planning to give me one day?"

"No!" She's red-faced, her eyes wide. "You don't understand. They haven't really told you how deep this goes, have they? How far back . . . I told your father he could work out partial custody in those other branches if he wanted, but I needed sole custody of you in the prime because this is what counts. You, here," she says.

And I'm flooded with memories of her—yes, she was in those other worlds, different versions of her. She was often scared. She worried about me. I was handed off between them at designated meeting places—parks, indoor McDonald's playgrounds; sometimes I was escorted on planes, flying cross-country. Those lives were different. She's right. My life has been fractured, too—and not just one life, but many.

And then it hits her. She spins quickly around, looking out the window over the sink and then back at me. "This isn't the prime." She quickly shakes her head and raises a finger. She doesn't want me to confirm it. She knows. She grabs my wrist, as if making sure I'm still really there. "I thought I could save you," she whispers.

"I never asked to be saved."

She starts crying, but she's angry too. "It's not the same, you know. It's never the same. It's not good to have all those lives to choose from. There's such a thing as a soul. When it comes to your father, I know which soul I fell in love with. How can you ever trust the person you love when sometimes they're there and sometimes they're not?"

How can you trust the person who doesn't tell you the truth about who you are? "No," I say. "No. You trust the person you love because you do."

She whispers, "I've lost you."

Maybe she's right, I think. Maybe I'm already gone. But I say, "No, you haven't lost me. I'm still here."

I hug her. She wraps her arms around me, holding on tight. I feel the shudder of a sob she's trying to hold down.

I whisper, "Don't tell Uncle Alex that I've created my own world. You can't trust him. In another world, he's captured Dad and is trying to get him to confess something, beating him. Alex could kill him."

She draws back and looks at me for a moment. "How dangerous is it for you now? Is someone after you?"

I can't tell my mother anything. It's now my job to protect her, not the other way around. "I'll be okay," I say. "Don't worry."

She smiles a tiny bit, as if she's trying to believe me.

"I need to know one thing," I say. "Did Dad ever mention an atlas? A specific one that he needed to hide?"

"He'd never tell me anything like that," she says. "It'd only make me a target. One reason he left is because he knew we'd be safer."

"What if he's still in love with you? What if he left but his heart—"

My mother reaches up and touches my cheek. "I still love his heart." And with a fierceness that surprises me, she says, "You can trust him with your life."

Though it seems to take all of her strength, she steps away from me. "Go on. I know you have to."

I stand there for just a second longer. I want to remember her like this—her hair loose around her face, her mascara smudged with tears. My mom. The two of us for so long, surviving.

"I'll check in on you in a bit if you want," she says. She means the other Alicia, the one of this world. The one who will maybe have ice cream with her later after I'm gone.

"Okay," I say.

CHAPTER FIFTEEN

MY ROOM looks exactly the same but somehow feels different.

The frosted window, the ancient wallpaper with small winding roses, yellowed at the seams. I feel a pang of homesickness even though I'm home.

There's a Plath poem about not being a mother, no more than a cloud could be a mother. I can't remember it exactly. Plath had two children; she sealed the door to their bedroom before she turned on the gas stove to kill herself. She was beautiful, her children were still very young. What did she think about as the small kitchen filled with gas? She had to believe what she was doing was the only option—the only ending she was allowed. And she had to think her kids would be better off without her. How else could she follow through with it?

I reach under the pillow on my bed and pull out my copy of Plath's poems. I stare at her picture for a moment; her face in dusty black and white, trapped in a small circle, forever. I touch the photograph. Every time I read one of Plath's poems, I want to say, "Don't do it. Don't kill yourself. Stay."

But maybe that's just what the poems are whispering to themselves.

Are mothers clouds that can blow away? I know my mother loves me, but how could she even think about letting Alex put me through some surgery that would take away part of who I am?

In the kitchen, she said, *It's not good to have all those lives to choose from.* She meant my father's worlds, but everyone has choices—endless choices. It's how lives are built.

She said, *How can you ever trust the person you love when sometimes they're there and sometimes they're not?*

That has nothing to do with universes. That's about trust, faith, the blind leap of falling in love.

Maybe my mother lived her life afraid of just being in love. It's unknowable, even without all those other worlds. Uncontrollable.

I apply pressure to my left hand. I have to find my father. I would be grateful to have any version of him.

I sit on the edge of my bed and grip my knees. My parents were really in love, and it seems like it was an immediate falling—and maybe a lasting love, despite the fact that they're no longer together. I've wanted to know this forever. Now I do and it feels like . . . what? It feels like hope. Not so much hope that they will get back together—no. I'm not that delusional. It's more that two people can fall in love at all. That's a hopeful thought, right? Love, it exists, and not just for people in books and movies or for poets doomed by it. Except my mother had been afraid to live with the reality of who my father was—is. My father, in the prime, fighting for his life.

Not a brute.

A good man who's had to make some hard choices.

I have infinite regrets, he said. *I keep one version of myself hidden away—the good one who's tried to do the right thing.*

The right thing.

The world where he didn't take my mother from Alex. The world where Alex and my mother are married; the world that's disintegrating.

In that world, did my father convince my mother to go back to Alex, to hide that she was pregnant with me, and let Alex believe I was his?

Alex must not know the way his life turned out in that world. If he knew there was a world where he did get to be with my mother, he wouldn't want that branch to die.

I sit up, wide-eyed.

Alex's perfect world exists and he doesn't know it. If he did, he would try to save it. I don't have the atlas but I do have something that he wants.

I have to tell Alex what he's destroying. He said there was another drug that they wanted to try on another branch. Wouldn't he try it on the dying branch if he knew the truth?

I remember my father's body fishhooked midair, beaten and bruised.

Who else even knows about the atlas?

I get up and stare at the dark window. Gemmy. So he must have chosen to give it to my father, not Alex. Gemmy's held it in his own hands. The buzzing rises again all over me: I'm lit up from the inside.

I open my top desk drawer and find my compass. But then I remember I promised Hafeez I'd write my other self a note.

I write on the back of my hand. *Hi, it's me. Call Hafeez.* And then I add: *Be good to Mom.*

Then I push the sharp tip of the compass into the flesh of my palm and blood rises. The times I've landed in Gemmy's world with the ancient bulldog, I've felt it in my upper arm, so I ignore the buzz in my right hand and grab my upper arm instead.

I close my eyes and remember what it was like when Gemmy grabbed me and hugged me—to have a grandfather, a real one, in a way I can really remember. For so long it's just been me and my mom, but now it's like my family is being brought back to me, one at a time.

I stare at the blood and think of the bulldog's crooked row of bottom teeth, Gemmy's boozy sweet smell, and then my arm starts to hurt. I grip it tightly, and the room jerks around me, as if popping loose piece by piece.

But just before it's gone, I reach into my pocket and grab the photo of Jane and Jax as a little boy. I pinch it between my thumb and knuckle, wondering if it can travel with me. Can I piggyback this one small thing?

The room dissolves . . . tiny pinpricks of light.

A pair of wide green eyes staring at me.

A girl's pale face and dark hair.

Behind her, wood-paneled walls, a rocking chair, windows full of night, the smell of cigars.

I've been staring into dark trees. That's my job here—to keep watch.

I'm holding something. I look down and there's the photograph of Jax and Jane. It came with me. So maybe Alex is right and I do have my father's ability to piggyback.

The girl, who's seven or so, starts whisper-singing: "Ticky hi, ticky ho. Ticky hi-dy hi-dy ho. . . ." She clicks one of her small nails against the glass of a hurricane lamp.

We're in a cabin. The bulldog is asleep on the floor, its back legs kicked out behind it.

I know we're safe, unless people appear in the woods or drive up the logging road.

I hear voices coming from a back room in the cabin.

"Where's Gemmy?" I ask the girl.

She startles and stares up at me. The hurricane lamp is under her chin, casting strange shadows on her face.

"Gemmy," I say. "Is he here? My grandfather?"

She backs away from me and drops the lamp. It falls, snuffing the wick. The room darkens, and she runs toward the voices and the distant light in a back room. "She's here! She's here!" she shouts.

I hear the scrape of chairs, heavy boots.

Gemmy, holding a flashlight, barrels into the room first. His thin white wisps of hair stick up on his head. "Is it you?"

I nod.

Three men and two women—all about Gemmy's age—file into the room after him. The women both wear their hair dyed dark and teased. One of the men has scoliosis that curves his back to one side. Another is bulbously fat, and the third is lean and tall, a black man with high cheekbones—I've seen his face before, but I can't place him. They all look at me expectantly.

"From the prime?" one of the women asks.

"Yes, yes, of course. Can't you tell?" Gemmy says.

"Who are all these people?" I ask Gemmy quietly. The bulldog is up and sniffing my boots.

"What?" asks the man with scoliosis. "You don't recognize us?"

"We been here all along," the other woman says in a rough, deep smoker's voice.

"What do you mean?" I ask.

"Search your memories, Alicia," Gemmy says. "We're your aunts and uncles. This here's Olsson, your godfather." He claps the tall, thin man on the back.

"You're Olsson. You were in the room with me and Jane," I say. "You were the one who gave the order to put me under again."

"Sorry about that. I play both sides. I work for Alex to keep a closer eye on him."

"What about Jane?"

"She does what she can," Olsson says, and then he takes a step toward me. "Don't you see us in those memories?"

I have seen him. I know he's been there. But I'm not sure if I can trust my memories.

"I'm your godfather, in every world your father's ever made," Olsson says.

"I'm not here for a reunion," I say. I still don't know if I should trust all of these people. "I'm here for the atlas."

"You can't hand it over to Alex," Gemmy says. "You know that."

The little girl sneaks back into the room, rounding the door frame.

"If I don't hand it over, Alex will kill my father," I tell him.

"The atlas is all that we are," Gemmy says. "Our history, our worlds. We're the living links. Each of us represents one of the old family lines, or what's left. We're the old guard, still fighting people like Alex, those who want to exploit branches, denying our collective humanity."

"Goddamned imperialists," the man with the bowed back mutters.

"We're the protectors of those worlds," Gemmy says.

"We've been called thugs, mobsters, rebels," Gemmy says. "We don't care what anyone calls us. We all got together here, waiting for you, Alicia."

"Why me?"

"You're one of us now."

A few smile and nod. The little girl leans against the wall, slides down, and sits there, staring at me.

"I need to know where the atlas is."

"We gave it to your father to hide—so none of us would know," Olsson says.

"Well, he doesn't know either," I say.

"If she ain't got her dad's gift, then none of it matters," says the man with the bowed back.

"What gift?"

"Piggybacking," Gemmy says.

"I've got the gift." I pull out the picture of Jax and Jane. "At least enough to bring this with me."

I hand the picture to Gemmy and the others gather around.

"My daughter," the heavy man says. "Jane and my grandson, Jaxy. I didn't make it in that branch. Died in the first wave of the epidemic." He holds the picture so tightly his hand trembles. Jane *is* Jax's mother, and this is his grandfather. Does Jax even know this man is alive, here?

"I told you she'd have the gift!" Gemmy says to the others. "That atlas was the last of its kind—or, well, the last that anyone seems to know of, and not many do. We destroyed all but one."

"If Alex gets it, he'll destroy all those branches," I say. "Right?"

"And these branches date way back," Olsson says. "We've got worlds where people who were assassinated in the prime got to live it out."

"You know how some researcher will come up with some cure for a disease almost by accident?" the woman with the smoker's voice says. "That's no accident. Someone in a branch who was never born in the prime figures it out. We transport the information, make it look like an accident. See?"

"Someone dies in the prime, someone like me," Gemmy says, "—well, sometimes they're alive somewhere else. See what that might mean to someone?"

"We can't predict the future any more than you can," Olsson says. "And we can't change the past. But being able to see how things play out in a world with just one tiny change is amazing. And sometimes horrifying."

Hafeez and I were right. I try to imagine all these other worlds at once—a world where Lincoln wasn't shot. Or Martin Luther King Jr. and John F. Kennedy and his brother Bobby. If spandrels lose someone they love, they have a chance at finding them again? All those cures . . .

I feel buzzing in my right hand. I grab hold of my left to stop it like Jax taught me.

"Your father locked the atlas away where no one would think to look," Olsson says. "He'd have been smart about it."

"Like where?" I ask, frustrated.

"The roots are 'lovely, dark and deep,' " says the man holding the picture.

Gemmy looks out the windows into the trees. "I've only been a few times, myself. Lost worlds where anything can happen. Worlds can swallow themselves whole. If he hid the atlas there, he had to have help. Our line can't navigate the roots."

The man holding the picture says, "Mine can." Does this mean Jane once could? And can Jax?

"Why are you all here holed up in a cabin?" I'm angry with all of them suddenly. "Why aren't you trying to save my father in the prime?"

"We'd get him out if we could, but we don't know where he is," Olsson says. "Alex is all over his security. We can't get anything from our sources."

"Alex showed me a glimpse of my father; he has a camera on him." I remember my father kicking the camera—the parting of the curtain. "He's in a hotel room. It had strange windows, like some of the panes were circular."

"Circular windows?" Olsson says.

"Only one hotel I know of like that," Gemmy says. "It was a prison a long time ago in Boston. Oculus. That's the name of the kind of circular window it's known for. It's got a few like that. The hotel is called The Liberty now."

"He's being tortured in one of the rooms in that hotel," I say. "He'll die there if we don't save him."

Gemmy shoves his hands into his pockets and stares at the floor. This is his son. I know he must feel as desperate as I do.

"You die in a branch, you can't go back to that branch. It's dead to you because you're dead inside of it." Olsson looks directly at me. "Have you noticed that there's a world of your father's that you haven't gone back to in a while?"

My vision quivers. I squint at Olsson and Gemmy, confused, but then I know which one. "The sinking cruise ship. The Russians in the hotel, stitching up my shoulder."

"They did it to put pressure on your dad to talk," Olsson says.

"They? You mean Alex?"

Gemmy nods. "I'm sorry. I'll never understand that boy. He wasn't right, even as a kid. He always thought we loved Ellington more. He didn't get it. He's sick, Alicia. He's got a sickness in him."

"I was killed by Alex's people . . . to send my father a message, to get him to say where the atlas is?"

Olsson nods. "Your prime consciousness wasn't there, so you didn't know it."

Gemmy looks away, rubbing his jaw.

"So my father knows they killed me in that world?" I ask.

"It broke him," Gemmy says. "Even though he knows you're still alive, death is death. A father losing a child is never right. When you live many lives, joy and love are multiplied but so are grief and suffering."

I didn't feel my own death, can't even imagine it, but I feel the punch of my father's loss. I take a minute to collect myself, and then I manage to ask, "But what if my prime consciousness had been there?"

"It's the closest you can get to death without dying," Olsson says. "It's like something is gone. An amputation. A branch is cut off from you forever."

"My father's already dead in one branch."

"Which one?" Gemmy asks.

"The world that's crumbling. The world where Alex is my—" I can't say it and I don't have to. "The one in that picture."

Olsson knows what world I'm talking about. "He's not dead in that world, Alicia. He's been cut."

"What?" That's what Jax meant by "one way of putting it" when I mentioned my father being dead in that world. Being cut is a kind of death. My mind is reeling. "Why would he do that?"

"Maybe he was trying to protect the atlas," Gemmy says. "But your father's not going to remember anything now that he's been cut like that. No way to really reach him."

"But he knew he was getting cut," I say. "He'd have had a tiny window of time to leave some kind of clue behind. He'd have thought ahead."

"And he wouldn't have told you to look for him in that world,"

Olsson says. "He just wants you safe, out of harm's way. You become a target if you know where the atlas is."

"I'm already a target. I'm cuffed to a bed in the prime. You know that, Olsson."

He spreads his hands as if to say "point taken."

"If I can promise the atlas, then I have some power," I tell Olsson. "What if I'm able to lure Alex away from the prime?"

I know his perfect world now. If I could prove it exists and piggyback him into it, he'd be convinced it's worth saving. Couldn't he try? He has access to the new vaccine they're going to try out in another branch. Why not that one?

"Sure," Olsson says, "But we can't let Alex get hold of the atlas!"

I know what I have to do. I punch the edge of the windowsill, hard enough to make my fist bleed. I take the photo from Jane's father and I push as hard as I can on the spot on my collarbone, the spot that will take me to Jax's world.

The edges of the room start to blur.

"Olsson, tell Alex to have the vaccine ready." I fix my eyes on the blood rising from the thin flap of skin. "The new one he was saving for another branch."

"Alicia!" my grandfather calls after me. "The Liberty Hotel! We'll make a plan to save him. You hear me?"

I do hear him, barely, but I can't respond. The room is breaking all around me, a loud tearing as it rips completely apart.

Soon all I hear is the little girl's high-pitched voice, louder now: "Ticky hi, ticky ho. Ticky hi-dy hi-dy ho. . . ."

I close my eyes and listen to the song shatter. Individual notes ring and ring and then fade to nothingness.

CHAPTER SIXTEEN

I **WAKE** up in my rich-kid bedroom in Jax's world, sleeping under the ragged canopy of my bed. My body feels bruised and bone-tired. Did I transfer into my sleeping self and keep sleeping? I feel rested, like I got a few hours.

It's morning but the sunlight is weak. The window is open. The curtains—dusty and frayed—billow inward. It's almost peaceful, but the low hum of my consciousness in this world is trying to tell me, urgently, that things have gone badly.

I hear a light snore and turn to see a little boy with dark hair and crooked bangs stuck to his sweaty forehead. He's curled up on the other side of the bed. I swing my feet to the floor. Jax is asleep against the wall. Did he fall asleep while trying to watch over us? I feel a strange twinge of jealousy. He wasn't watching over *me*—he was watching over another me.

The night comes back to me in pieces. Men with guns in the quarantine camp. "Takers"—that's what Jax called them, gangs that have risen up from the chaos.

Pynch shot a man who'd been holding a baseball bat. He shot the bat first, which shattered; I remember the man's shocked expression and then Pynch shot him in the chest.

Jax was there with this little boy. We ran across a barren field.

I go to the window. The truck that Jax was driving when Pynch and I stole the medicine is parked in the street. A Humvee is parked on the lawn, but I don't see any guards. One door is wide open as if it's been abandoned. Is my mother still alive? Some part of me knows she is. Is Alex here?

The other houses seem to stare out at the street vacantly. Two have started to tilt toward each other as if there's a sinkhole opening up between them.

Someone calls my name from below.

It's Pynch, sitting on the steps to the house, cradling his rifle, looking up. Has he been keeping watch, too?

"You okay?" I ask.

He nods, then glances toward the master bedroom window, and I know Alex and my mother are in there, probably still sleeping. "Everyone's safe," he says. "The takers have cleared out." He looks a little hollow. His face blank.

"Thanks," I say.

"For what?"

I'm not sure. I only remember patches. "For everything. And standing guard too."

He shrugs. "I wouldn't have been able to sleep."

I nod and dip back inside. I don't want to wake Jax, but when I turn, he's standing up.

"I'm sorry," Jax says.

"About what?" I should tell him that I'm here, but I don't want to miss a confession.

He sits on the edge of the bed and starts tying his boot slowly, like he doesn't want to look at me. "Last night. I like you, I really do, but just not—"

"Wait." I can't let him go on. I'm afraid something happened between us—him and the other me. I have a feeling he's about to tell me he doesn't feel the same way I do. I don't want to hear it. "It's me. The other me."

He looks up, startled. "Oh," he says, and then he looks away.

"Who's the kid?" I point at the little boy, trying to change the subject even further away from whatever happened—or didn't happen—between us.

"Biddy—that's his nickname." And in an instant, I know Biddy had a twin sister who died a while ago. He hasn't gotten over it. Jax takes care of him. They're each other's family now. And I know the Alicia in this world loves that about them because her own family life is weirdly empty and always has been.

"My father," I say. "My real father. He isn't dead, is he? He got cut."

Jax nods.

"How bad is it?"

"He doesn't know he's your father. He doesn't even know he's a spandrel anymore." He walks to the window. "And I guess he isn't."

"Why? Why did he do it?"

"He should be the one to tell you all of this, but he can't." Jax closes his eyes, and when he opens them, he seems to be focused on something beyond me. "My mother and your father were friends. My mother always told me this world was your father's world. That he'd created it, trying to do the right thing." He runs one hand over the curtain's ruffle. Some of it turns to dust that flits and is gone. "Apparently, when your mother got pregnant with you, he worried he wouldn't be a good father."

I think of my mother in the kitchen, all the ways she tried to protect me. My father was trying, too, in his own way.

"So in this world, he convinced your mother to go back to your uncle while there was time for Alex to believe you were his."

Jax looks at me for a moment, letting me take this in. I bite the inside of my cheek to keep from crying. I'm struggling to keep myself together. The buzzing starts in my right hand like some kind of instinct to run away. But I push on the spot on my left hand. I'm not leaving.

"You know, for the record, your uncle is a good guy—at least here. He gave up studying spandrels after you were born. He got a job down here and moved with your mom and you from Boston. He got my mom a job in the same facility. Things were good for a while."

It's surreal, finding out your parents are real people. They made big decisions and had to live with them—in more than one world. I sit down on the edge of the bed, careful not to wake Biddy.

"Are you okay?" Jax asks.

"Yeah. It's just that my parents had good intentions but they screwed things up, and that's why I'm here at all."

"Me too," he says.

"What do you mean?" I ask.

"In the prime, my mom got pregnant by some guy, another grad student," he says. "The guy took off."

"I'm sorry." I know how he feels. For most of my life, I thought my father had abandoned me.

"It's okay. My mom and I were close. She made up for it."

Biddy kicks the sheets and coughs. Jax walks around the bed, touches the boy's head. "Shhh. It's okay."

Biddy settles back to sleep, and Jax pulls the sheet over his legs. "When my mother found out she was pregnant, she asked your dad for help. Because she was scared of Alex." It shocks me to hear him refer to Alex by name—especially because the Alex he's talking about is not the one who's here. He's the one I've known all my life, in the prime. "Alex was pissed. In that world, your mother had left him. He'd started talking about studying the children of spandrels—especially the ones with rare abilities. My mother didn't know where that research was going, but she knew I'd be a target."

He sits at the foot of the bed. "So she hid her pregnancy and, toward the end, she told Alex she had to be with her mother who was sick. She had me at her mother's house. And your father came and took me with him, into what was, at the time, a better, safer world that he'd just created." Jax clears his throat. His voice sounds frayed, dust choked. "My mother was also in this world—not her prime self, but still my mother."

I think of Jane. In the prime, she lost what mattered to her most. She'd kept the picture of her other self, raising her son all this time. No wonder she'd gotten cut. She could see her son but couldn't hold him. But I also imagine Jane in this world, being told the story, that a baby was coming from the prime—her own—and what it must have felt like to hold him for the first time, a kind of falling in love. This is the way my mother told me it felt when the nurses handed me as an infant to her, a headlong rush of immediate love. "But also protectiveness," my mother would always add. "I knew I'd do anything to keep you safe."

I stand up, reach into my pocket, and pull out the photograph of him and his mother. I hand it to him.

He looks at it and then up at me. "What's this?"

"I found it in your mother's desk drawer. In the prime. Maybe my father brought it to her."

He takes it. His hands are trembling. He shakes his head. "No.

The soul is the soul. My mother is dead. The one who gave me up might still be alive, but I don't know her."

"What if there's a way to stop it from getting worse, to rebuild this world? Remember the tree?"

He shakes his head. "It's all too far gone."

"If I can get the atlas, I might be able to trade it for a new vaccine."

"Alicia, it's too late. The best I can do is take care of the people who are left."

"I have to try. And I need to get to my father—the one who's here—and see if he can help me. If he can tell me how to get to the right world, then you could navigate from there, right?"

"He won't know."

"I need to at least talk to him."

We look at each other for a long moment. I want him to say something, anything. But all I see is the deep sadness in his eyes. I can't stand it. I walk to the door. "Then I'll find him myself. I have to keep trying."

"I won't be here when you get back. I'm going into Houston for more supplies."

I look at him—maybe for the last time. "It's too dangerous." Part of me knows that the takers come from the city.

He walks over to me, and for a second I'm charged with hope, but then he hands me the picture. "Here. Take it."

"It's yours."

"No, it's not."

I refuse to take it. "Keep it."

"I'm being practical, Alicia. We need to survive as long as we can. That's where I'm putting my energy. Nothing else."

Biddy sits up and rubs his eyes. "Jax?" he says. "Are we okay?"

Jax shoves the picture in my jacket pocket and walks over to Biddy, brushes his hair back from his forehead.

As I head for the hallway, I hear Jax saying, "Don't worry. Don't worry now."

CHAPTER SEVENTEEN

DOWN THE mansion's dark hallway, I find my way to the stairs. I want to turn around and tell Jax I was wrong and he was right, just to stay with him a little longer. But I can't. I have to figure out where my father lives—the father who doesn't know he's my father, the man who might know where the atlas is, even if he doesn't know that he knows.

I walk down the hall and pass the master bedroom doorway.

I see my mother propped on the bed, sleeping, her breathing labored.

Weak sunlight is blocked by cardboard duct-taped over the windows. I step closer to the bed, afraid to make a sound. Her dark hair fans across the pillow, and I smell something familiar. Lilac. The powder she loves. Eyes closed, she drags in another pained breath.

An IV line runs up to a metal tree; a line of bottles and syringes clutter the bedside table. I walk to her bedside, reach for her hand, begin to kneel down beside her, and then a lamp switches on behind me.

I stand up and turn so fast I almost fall backward.

Alex is sitting in a tufted armchair against the wall, holding a newspaper. A pile of them sits on the floor beside him. He's wearing gray pajamas, glasses perched on his nose. This Alex has a little more paunch, more wrinkles around the eyes. His hair's thinner on top. Behind him in the corner is a set of golf clubs. One of the clubs rests against the arm of his chair within easy reach.

Alex folds his newspaper and leans back, looking at me. "Sorry I startled you," he says. "I was looking back to see if I could trace where we went wrong."

A *Houston Chronicle* headline reads DEATH TOLL RISES. The issue is almost two years old. The ink is smudged, the paper yellowed. Next to the piles of newspapers, I notice the base of the lamp: the cord has been cut, the wires inside spliced into a car battery. The horror of this place—it all seems contained in that frayed newspaper, the dark gleam of the battery, my mother unconscious in the bed.

I remind myself that in this world Alex is a good man. "We were lucky last night. We've been so lucky for so long." He rubs his face.

There is nothing I can say. He had everything he wanted in this world, only to watch it fall apart. I actually feel sorry for him. "I've got to go."

"The guards have abandoned us. Please stay here."

"I won't be long."

He seems too defeated to argue or try to stop me. I pause in the doorway, look back at my mother. Even as sick as she is, she's beautiful. I wonder if she found some happiness in this life, before all of this started.

Alex stands unsteadily and hugs me. I can't believe it. I make myself hug him back, tell myself this Alex is a different man. He lets me go and says, "Be safe, my girl."

"I promise." I'm not his girl, but I am. I know he watches me as I walk out the door.

At the bottom of the stairs, I see some cards and pictures on the narrow table behind the sofa. I pick up a holiday card, furry with dust. I rub it clean. This one's of my mother, Alex, and me, smiling in ski gear, a snowy mountain behind us. My hair is very blond—some cheerleader look I'm apparently trying to rock in this world. It reads: *Happy Holidays from the Maxwells!*

I fold the card, slip it in my back pocket, a little proof of this family for Alex in the prime.

I head for the kitchen, opening drawers until I find a phone book. The Greater Houston Area guide is three years old.

As I pull it out, I wonder how many of the people listed in it are long dead. I flip to the M's. I find Alex and Francesca Maxwell first. And then my father, Ellington Maxwell, in another column on the same page—1906 Thorn Lane. As I tear it out, the page frays but manages to remain intact. I fold it and stick it in my pocket with the holiday card.

I walk out the front door.

There's Pynch, still on the stoop.

"Do you have any gas in the truck?" I say. "I have a favor to ask."

He takes me in for a second, turns away, and says, "You're the other one, right? Jax told me. I can tell the difference between you and, well, you. You're a little less stuck-up."

"Uh, thanks," I say, walking down the steps. "Can you take me to Thorn Lane? Do you know where that is?"

"I know it but . . ." Pynch squints at me. "All of Thorn Lane could be gone by now. There are a lot sinkholes over there, crater pockets just under the top layers of dirt."

"My father's there. I have to get to him. I mean, I hope we can."

Pynch smiles. "Hope." He stands up and ruffles my hair. "Adorable." And I'm pretty sure he's blowing me off, but then he starts walking to the truck.

I run to the passenger door. "Thanks, Pynch. I mean it."

"No problem. We all die somewhere doing something."

His words chill me, but I climb in, settle on the cracked seat. As the truck starts to pull away, I look up at the upstairs windows, and I see Jax—for just a second—at the torn, gauzy curtains in my room, before he turns away.

Pynch drives through what looks like a suburban neighborhood planted in a cow field. Tall wooden fences ring the houses, all of them roofed with curved clay tiles. All of them dark.

"So I'm going to make a run to the camp and check on people," he says to me, slowing to a stop and propping the rifle on his lap. He scans, looking for movement, and I realize I'm doing it, too. "And then I'll come back for you. Keep an eye out for me."

"Okay," I say, reaching for the handle.

"If I was you, I'd get to the door as fast as you can."

"Thanks for the ride. I'll be as quick as I can." I jump out and run past a stunted tree to the gate. My father—cut? I'm scared to find out what's left of him. I keep running until I reach the door.

The house is completely dark, like all the others—with boarded windows. It's so still and empty it's hard to believe anyone ever lived here. I knock loud and fast, and the wood splinters a little. From inside, I hear shuffling, scraping, something being shoved aside.

"Dad?" I say, and all movement inside stops. I realize my mistake. "Uncle Ellington?"

"Alicia?" It's my father's voice, no question.

"Yeah! It's me!"

The door opens, and there's my dad. I'm startled by the way he looks. His cheeks are sallow and sunken, his hair almost entirely gray. He wears a rumpled button-down shirt over faded jeans. I see the tattoos, inching down one hand, another curling around his neck. "What are you doing here?" he says. He pulls the door wider. "Come in—hurry!"

I step inside. He shuts the door and shoves a scuffed-up bureau in front of it.

In the little bit of light coming through the boarded windows, I make out a small living room, two chairs, a sagging couch, a coffee table piled with books.

And sketches, dozens of them, taped to the walls. They are all variations on a theme: branches and vines, like the trees I used to doodle in my notebooks. But these are massive, drawn on several taped-together sheets. They twist and overlap in elaborate patterns, covering the walls.

"Why are you here?" he asks. "You should be at home."

"Listen, I have to tell you something, and I need you to hear me out."

He gives a hesitant nod. "What is it?"

"It's been a few years now since you got cut, right?"

He stares at me, blinking, as if he's not sure what I mean.

I try again. "The operation. So you wouldn't be able to jump or see other worlds."

He gives me a smile, and for a moment, I can sense the father I've glimpsed from world to world—sometimes haggard, sometimes exhausted, but a raw power running through him, an animal cunning. But what he says next shakes me to the bone. "You always were a jokester, Ali-gal. Always coming up with crazy stories."

Ali-gal? The nickname is probably buried inside of me some-where. I wonder if I'll ever get used to this fragmented existence. "I'm not joking," I say.

My father looks genuinely concerned. "Are you okay? Did you get your last round of shots?"

Of the worthless vaccine? "You did have an operation, didn't you?"

"I did," he says rubbing the back of his skull. "A lesion. They had to go in so the cancer wouldn't spread."

"It wasn't cancer!" I tell him.

He doesn't believe me.

I point at the wall. "How about these sketches? Don't you know what they are?"

"Just a way to pass the time."

I get up, pull one of them from the wall. "This doesn't remind you of your tattoos?" I set the sketch on the cluttered coffee table.

My father shrugs. "The tattoos were just for fun. I was pretty stupid back in the day."

I feel like I could scream. I try to keep my voice calm. "Are you lying, or do you really just not remember?"

He sits down on the couch. His entire body sags. "There's a lot I don't remember. Your dad's been good to me. Francesca too. He offered to take me in, but I never want to be a burden. You know?"

That's how I felt before I knew I was a spandrel, why I almost leaned into that knife. "Do you remember anything about an at-las?" I ask.

"An atlas?"

"You're going to have to try to remember. You hid it and I have to find it." I pace a few seconds and then sit down in the chair across from him, lean forward. I take a deep breath. "First of all, you should try to remember that you are my father," I say. "You used to know this. You have to believe me."

He closes his eyes, shakes his head slowly.

I rush on. "You created this world to do right by me and Mom, but also because you lost faith in yourself. Maybe you were trying to be another, better version of yourself. You said that to me once."

My father looks at me with a sadness I recognize: it's the same expression he had in the backyard looking at my mother. I know some part of what I'm saying rings a distant bell.

"Okay, I'm going to tell you something else, something that happened before I was born, something I'm sure you or my mother or Alex would never have told me."

"Ali-gal," he says, "don't stir up ancient history."

"You were in love with my mother, Francesca, once, weren't you? And you knew I was yours. You made a hard decision. Don't tell me you've forgotten that."

"Alicia—" my father says, trying to slow me down, but I won't stop now.

"No, listen." I lean so close to my father that our knees are almost touching. "You said the first time you saw her, you were sure that this was the face of the woman who'd break your heart in a million ways."

My father raises his head, stares at the wall covered in his drawings of winding and twisting branches.

"Maybe you left me a note about the atlas before your operation." I stand up. "Maybe something's hidden here."

"No," my father says, shaking his head. "There's nothing."

"All of these drawings of branches," I say. "Your brain, some deep-down part, is trying to tell you something."

"They aren't branches," Ellington says.

"Of course they are!"

"No," my father says. "Some reach up like branches or out, but, in my head, they're all underground. They're all roots."

I freeze. *Roots.* My father has been drawing roots. "What was the last tattoo you got before the operation?"

He shakes his head. "It was just stupid. I got it on a whim. It doesn't even go with the others I've gotten."

"What is it?"

He takes off a boot, pulls down the sock, and shows me a tiny orange sun near his ankle.

I think of the images on Hafeez's phone. This is it. The body trigger to the roots has to be next to the anklebone. "Blood," I say to my father. "The mind trigger into your worlds is always blood." I grab his wrist and show him all of the fine nicks on his skin. "Did you cut yourself?"

He shakes his head. "A bad habit when I was younger. I don't anymore."

"If too many people knew your mind trigger, if they were breaking into your worlds, you'd have to have made a different one. And this is it. The sun."

He reaches out and cups my chin. "Alicia," he says.

"What?"

He hugs me and then he whispers, "I miss you." And I know what he means—he misses knowing, he misses his daughter, he misses his other worlds. . . .

"Thank you," I whisper.

"For what?" he asks.

"You have no idea what you had to give up."

We both hear the rattle of an engine coming closer, and he looks through a crack in the boarded windows.

"Truck out there."

"Pynch is back." I walk to the door, and he drags back the dresser, unlocks the bolt for me.

With the drawings of roots behind him—twisting and spiraling—it seems like they've sprouted from his body.

"I know one thing," my father says.

"What's that?"

"No matter what, family is family." Does this mean he believes that I'm his daughter, on some level?

I hug him again. "I love you," I say.

"I love you too," he says.

And whether he knows he's my father or not doesn't matter. I got everything I came for.

CHAPTER EIGHTEEN

IN THE truck Pynch is silent, his jaw clenched. I guess things weren't good at the camp. I decide it's better not to ask.

I look out the window at the blighted blur of landscape rolling by. Mostly craters, swirling with dust.

On one hand, I feel kicked in the gut—seeing my father like that, burnt out, lost to himself—but on the other, it was like some part of my father, deep down, was there and acknowledged me, his daughter. I was sure my father had given up on me, so maybe I was just hungry for anything fatherly from him. In the prime I grew up feeling starved for his love. And I never realized what that feeling was until I saw him.

I'm also elated. I got what Jax needs to get me into the roots where the map is hidden—mind and body triggers.

"I need Jax's help," I say.

"He's gone, left Biddy with your dad and headed for Houston."

"He couldn't have gotten far." I feel a buzz spreading through my body, zeroing in on my hand. I reach down and press hard on the opposite pressure point to keep myself here.

"He took the Humvee."

"Hey," I say to Pynch. "Will you—"

"No."

"I might be able to get a cure. Maybe we can still turn things around here."

"I grew up around here and I had a pretty happy childhood," Pynch says. "My parents both died in the second wave of the epidemic. I lost my sister in the third. The waves kept coming. A couple years ago, I was playing baseball on scholarship." He glances up at the sky. "I have no illusions about how this is going to end."

"I've got a shot at this. It's not a great shot, but it's something," I say. "And I need Jax."

Pynch's face is stony.

"Come on," I say. "Everybody's got to die somewhere doing something."

He glances at me, gives a grunt, and then turns the wheel, and I know we're headed into the city.

Pynch drives past the gates of the quarantined camp. It's vacant, not a soul in sight, but some sections are smoldering. A few yards ahead, he guides the truck onto a razor-straight two-lane road. In the rearview mirror, I see the camp sign: SJ RECOVERY CENTER, DISTRICT 15, AREA 108.

"So this was where people went to try to survive," I say.

Pynch nods. "You'll find bullshit lives on even in the worst of times."

We pass a huge billboard for Sienna Plantation rocked back as if someone tried to bulldoze it and gave up, and then we cross an intersection with a highway. It stretches before us, cracked and empty except for a few wrecked and deserted cars.

On the roadside, there's a body, bloated from dehydration and rotting in the sun.

"God forgive us all," Pynch says then, his voice hoarse. "For whatever we did to deserve this."

"Nobody here did anything to deserve this."

He looks back and forth around the horizon, scanning, always scanning. "You know I got the truck because I was a guard. It was my job to dump dead bodies into the mass graves. After my family was all gone"—he coughs, spits out the window—"after that, these survivors were my family. Jax, his mother, Biddy, all of them. The other guards hightailed it when they had the chance. But I stuck around."

The sky above us is the brightest blue I've seen.

"How did you survive?" I say.

"I must have a natural immunity in me, somewhere. A tiny percentage of the population had it. But maybe that's not the kind of surviving you're talking about. Maybe you mean how did the ones still around not go crazy."

"You and Jax seem to have kept it together."

"We have a purpose. That's why he doesn't want to go with you."

I wonder if Pynch knows what happened between the other me and Jax last night. I think about asking but stop myself. I don't really want to know.

"Where should I look for him?"

Pynch sighs. "He'll be around the hospitals. Pretty much what's left of the civilized world is on military bases and warships. There are a few in the Gulf. They still send some supplies to the hospitals, the ones that could barricade themselves good enough." Pynch angles into the oncoming lane to avoid several wrecked cars. He doesn't bother to switch back. "Going off-road for a bit."

He swings the truck into a field. We're driving alongside a canal for a while, and then we're back on a road again. It widens into a highway lined by dead strip malls, bone-white and bare in the sun.

I try to concentrate on my other self, Alicia in the world where I didn't take the gun. I don't jump into my other world. I just try to catch a glimpse.

I see a window with one pane covered with cardboard, taped into place. Jane's office. Jane is sitting next to me on the sofa, not in her chair where she usually sits. She's holding my hand. She's talking about an operation. My mother—she's there, too. She's pacing, too anxious to sit down. She's nodding along to what Jane's telling me.

Cut? In that world, are they trying to talk me into getting cut?

I feel sick. I don't want to think about it. I can't. No one would really go through with it. *I* wouldn't go through with it. Or would I? I'm a different person there now. Completely different.

I stare out at the ghostly Texas landscape—gaping holes where storefront windows used to be, divots in the earth that yawn open into pits.

Pynch points ahead. "You'll follow this road. But not *on* the road, you understand me?" He looks over at me.

I don't know what I should be afraid of, which only makes me more afraid. I nod.

"Head straight for about a mile. Go under the loop—the freeway. At the fork, bear right. You'll see a big stadium on Old Spanish Trail, but I don't know if there are signs anymore. After you cross Greenbrier, you'll see a hospital on the right. Start there. There's another one just southeast of that. And Shriner's to the north, about a mile. Follow Fannin Street for that one. Not on the street, right? Stay out of sight."

"Right, okay," I say, but I'm not sure if I have it all. All of these roads should be familiar to me—the Alicia who grew up here. But I don't recognize anything.

"He'll be on foot by now. The Humvee would just make him a target."

"Got it."

"It might look like the place is deserted, but it's not."

Stretched before me are malls, industrial parks, and weed-seamed parking lots dotted with decaying cars, all flattened under the heavy sky. I can't tell if the day is already fading or if it's just the darkening clouds.

Pynch takes us to an overpass, and I see a church on the right, Iglesia de los Santos, hand-painted in red on a peeling street sign. Church of the Saints—Señor Fernandez would be proud. His classroom feels like worlds away, and it is.

"Saint Pynch," I mutter under my breath. I know better than to say it loudly enough for him to hear.

We bump along, the grass almost as high as the truck doors. The engine strains, but Pynch makes it through and wedges us into the trees, cutting the engine. We sit for a moment, listening, but there's nothing beyond the sound of wind.

He gives me some water, one of his MREs, pulls out a heavy plastic bag, and tosses it to me. "Dump your stuff in there. You can knot it at the top, keep your hands free."

I do what he tells me to, and when I look up, Pynch is holding a knife out to me, the curved tip of the blade pointed down. "Wish I had something better to give you, but I'm fresh out."

I take the knife. "Thanks." I don't want Pynch to know how scared I am, so I reach for the door handle like I'm in a hurry to go.

Pynch doesn't seem fooled. "Listen. There's a place not far from here that I'll stop at tomorrow. Jax will know where it is. I'll get you guys back out of here, hopefully."

The "hopefully" makes me nervous. "I'll see you again soon," I say, as if I'm asking him to make me a promise.

"I don't say good-bye to people." Pynch glances at the sky through his windshield. "So good luck."

I slide out of the cab, slam the door, watch Pynch back out and head for the road. I can hear the truck engine for a long time after it disappears beyond the rise of the overpass. Soon, the only sound is the dry grass bending and ticking around me.

CHAPTER NINETEEN

CLOUDS ARE rolling in over Houston's pocked and empty streets. Thunder in the distance, the afternoon light dimming.

I slide the bag over my shoulder, knife in hand, and head for the parking lot of the next shopping center. I move from one spot of cover to another—a fallen awning, a rusted Dumpster. I feel a flash of hope when I see a towering sign at one entrance that reads MAIN MEDICAL CENTER.

I pass a Carefree Inn with a mattress in front of the smashed office door.

With each step I'm listening and watching for movement, but there's only the soft, wet wind, the smell of brine.

The rain comes just as I make it to the overpass. I scan ahead, taking a moment to catch my breath.

I move on and quickly get rain soaked. More sidewalks lined with small, ragged, dying trees, dwarfed against the huge bowl of sky, the six-lane road and football field–size parking lots. Cars are scattered like abandoned toys.

Taquerias, pharmacies, fast-food joints, gas stations with their nozzles on the ground, and an ice cream parlor, somehow sadder than all the other places with its faded sign hanging by one hinge over the dark doorway.

I run through another major intersection. Rain is streaming down my face and neck. There's a hulking spaceship-like stadium up ahead. The Astrodome?

After another intersection, I see a hint of a skyline and come to a split in the road. The sky is almost black with rain, and the shapes of the buildings ahead seem ghostlike. I hope this is the fork in the road that Pynch meant.

Soon I'm in a neighborhood that looks expensive—or used to be. Two military trucks rumble by, and I hide behind a dead hedge.

Then I hear a voice.

I freeze.

Now two voices are talking low.

"You go around," one says.

Then, "Get her."

I start running, the rain needling my face.

I can hear the wet smack of footsteps behind me, my plastic sack slapping my back. I don't look back.

I hear a grunt as someone stumbles. I could be killed here. The fear rises in me, tightens my chest.

I charge through another intersection, instinctively looking for traffic, but of course there's none—just the black, slick street and the large buildings ahead, closer now. I swerve past a bunkerlike building on the right, and the sign by the road—MEDICAL SUITES— and crash through another hedge. Around the corner of the building, I find a spot to crouch.

I clutch the knife and wait, sending a silent thank-you to Pynch for it.

"Come on out, girl," the man says, his voice low. "We know

you're here." I make out bare feet, a tangle of hair, a crowbar clutched in a man's fist.

Through the tangle of bushes, I make out another figure running toward him. "Let's go! We can't hold this area."

"She's here somewhere, I know it," the first man says.

"We're going," the other man says.

The first man bangs the crowbar on a concrete pillar. "Get you later," he says to me, and then they run off.

For the next couple of hours, I move like someone under fire. My progress is a series of dashes from point to point. I make it through another huge intersection—Greenbrier, one of the streets Pynch mentioned.

Finally I see huge white buildings surrounded by endless over-grown lawns and parking lots. I feel a wave of despair when I think of trying to find Jax in all this. And who knows if this is the hospital he chose? This is a city of hospitals. Or is he already heading back, and I've missed him?

I might never see him again.

I feel sick about it. I knew I had a crush on him, but this is when it hits me that it's more than a crush. I'm crazy about him. I didn't want to hear what happened last night and how I'm not his type. I know that's what was coming. He doesn't like me back. I look up at the sky and wonder how long I've really felt this way. From the beginning? Was that the weird charge I felt when I first saw him in the courtyard before I even really knew him? Is that kind of thing even possible?

But it doesn't matter when it started. I know it's the truth, and I know why I've denied it so long—because all I know about falling for someone is that it will screw up your life.

I tell myself to forget it, to try to unfeel how I feel. But I know that's a waste of effort.

Hoping to find a safe spot to watch for Jax, I make my way to a parking deck and climb the spiraling entrance. The sky is clearing. Six levels up, I look out across the city—the glass towers of downtown in a wash of late-afternoon glow seem to waver in and out of view. I blink, rub my eyes, but the buildings still twist like streamers as the clouds pull apart in the shifting light.

There are movements here and there, people foraging.

A woman hurries across the street, dragging her small child by the hand.

An old man seems to look straight at me from the brush edging the parking lot below and then slips out of sight.

A scream that could've come from a cat rises, and then nothing. The quiet unnerves me.

I move to the edge of the concrete barrier, trying to see.

Another movement: someone dips between the shadows of two buildings, running fast and soundlessly—hunched over, carrying something?

He's heading away from me, and when he turns, I see his canvas backpack, the gloss of his dark hair.

Jax.

CHAPTER TWENTY

I GRAB my bag and, holding the knife, I plunge back down the spiral staircase, terrified Jax might get away before I can catch sight of him again.

I force myself to do a quick sweep of the open ground between me and the buildings, then sprint across, straight toward the darkened passageway I saw him heading for. I make it into the shadows.

I don't see him.

He's gone.

I wonder if it's worth the risk to call out for him. I open my mouth, then stop hard.

Jax steps out from behind a dented metal door, a Taser aimed at my chest. It's dark; the only light's behind me, and so there's a good chance he can't see who I am.

"Drop the knife," he says. Those bright blue eyes on me, he ticks the Taser toward the ground to indicate what he wants. His face is taut, determined. If he's afraid, I can't tell.

I drop the knife; it clatters on the cement, the sound startling us both. "It's me," I say. "Alicia."

He takes another step closer and lowers the Taser. "Jesus, don't sneak up on people."

"I didn't mean to scare you."

"I wasn't scared," he says, but he lets a whistle of air out through his teeth.

I think of my father standing in the frozen backyard, telling me how he knew he'd seen the face of the woman who would break his heart in a million ways. Is that what my father has to teach me about falling in love? I feel like I'm seeing the face of someone who will only break my heart. I hope it doesn't have to be in a million ways, and all I can think of is how badly, and in how many worlds, is this going to hurt?

He sticks the Taser in the back pocket of his jeans, shifts his backpack from one shoulder to the other. It looks heavy, landing hard against his back. "How'd you find me?"

"Pynch got me as close as he could."

"He can be a real softy," he says and then he looks away. "Did you talk to your father?"

"I got the trigger, mind and body."

For a second, he's impressed. It's just a quick flash across his face. "Good for you."

"So what happens to someone who can't navigate the roots and tries to go in alone?"

"They can't see anything. It's only blackness, or sometimes they only see a reflection of their own fears. What are you afraid of?"

I'm afraid of my father being beaten to death in a hotel room. I'm afraid of never seeing Jax again, losing him. "Right this minute?" I say. "I'm afraid of you."

"Me?"

"If you don't help me, it's over. Everything I've been trying to do—gone."

"The atlas will only give your uncle more power. Is that what you want?"

"If I can get my hands on it, I might be able to strike some deals. This world isn't going to last much longer. Perception is every-thing—you said that—and eventually this branch is going to die just like the side of that tree that nobody looks at, and soon there just won't be enough of you left to keep holding it together, right? Unless I can get a vaccine, unless—"

Then we hear footsteps.

Jax lifts his hand, freezes, raising the Taser. He pulls me around a corner, a darkened emergency exit sign above us. But the exit is locked and we're trapped in a small closet-size space. Pressed against each other, we don't move.

The only light streams from the jagged hole in the door where the lock was ripped out.

I open my mouth to ask him what's going on, and he presses a finger to my lips. A jolt of energy surges through me. I can barely breathe.

More footsteps overhead, some running and some deliberate, pa-trolling.

A strange hooting noise, answered by another farther off.

I can feel him breathing, the rise and fall of his ribs against mine. His mouth is beautiful, so close.

The footfalls grow louder until they're pounding overhead and then, just as fast as they came, they're gone.

We wait a bit longer. I'm in no rush to move. He looks at me and whispers, "The root worlds I see are strange and beautiful, and sometimes they're dangerous."

Does this mean he's thinking of helping me? I'm scared to ask. "For a long time, I thought I was crazy," I say. "Everyone let me think I was losing it so that I wouldn't ever know the truth."

"Are you glad you know the truth?" His blue eyes shine.

I nod. "Everything I thought I was hallucinating was real," I whisper. "Even you."

We could move away from each other now. The footsteps are long gone. We don't move, and I think about what it'd be like if we were two kids at a school dance. It's quiet. And it's no longer like we're pressed together but leaning against each other. Can he hear how loudly my heart is beating? Even though this is one of the most dangerous places I've been in my life, I feel safe.

"People here kept dying and dying, and I feel like it's killed something in me too," he says. "It was like finding yourself alone in a house as a little kid. You can run from room to room, calling for someone—but they're gone, and you begin to realize that they left no note and they aren't coming back."

I know he's been scarred by everything he's been through, but just as he can't forget all that's been lost, I can't forget all that is still at stake. "We can try to save the ones still here. We can at least try."

"This world you're looking for, it's an offshoot of your father's imagination. My mother told me about it. She told me where to look once we got there. She explained it all, and it's, well, are you sure you want . . . ?"

"I'm not sure of anything, but I'm not scared." And it's the truth. For some reason—maybe because I'm with him—I feel resolved.

"Okay," he says, and he steps out of the small space and slides his backpack onto the floor. I put my plastic bag next to it.

"It's your father's branch, so you'll have to be the one—"

"To piggyback you in. I know." He steps out of the small space and leads me back the way we came, checking in all directions. It's clear.

"There's just one thing about that," I confess. "I've never actually piggybacked another human being before."

"What have you piggybacked?" he says, looking up at the sky, which shifts like layers of gauze, like something unraveling.

"Well, that picture I showed you."

"What else?"

"That's it."

He stares at me. "Do you know what happens to someone if they get lost when someone's trying to piggyback them into another branch?"

"No, what?"

"I've heard it's just wind and darkness. You can hear voices but you can't call back to them. You're just *gone*."

"I'll hold on tight. I promise." I wonder, though, if this is in my control. I hope so. "I'll hold on with everything I've got."

"Here," Jax says, pointing to a spot against a building, out of view of the street. "You sit here. I'll wrap my arms around you."

My heart is a drum in my ears. I sit on his legs as he leans against the wall.

"Where's the spot?"

I touch the skin just above the small knot of his anklebone. "Here."

He grips his ankle and with the other arm holds me around the waist. I lock my arms around his neck. I can feel his soft breaths.

"The sun," I say.

"The sun," he whispers.

I stare at a reflection of the sun, glinting off a puddle. Pieces of buildings and concrete fall away, the world breaking apart, and then, suddenly, brightness . . .

And then weight, pressing air from my chest. My muscles start to burn. I can't breathe. My body can't bear the pressure—from within and bearing down on me. I'm sure that I'm going to be torn to shreds. Explode . . . and then . . .

I hear a voice. Jax, his voice rough and raw and breathless, whispers, "It's okay. I can see it. We're almost there. . . ."

CHAPTER TWENTY-ONE

A COLD floor, quiet and dark. I'm holding Jax. He's holding me. We start to cough. The piggybacking took my breath. I feel weak, wrung out. "We made it!"

He hushes me.

We both get to our feet. We're in a dimly lit hall lined with mirrors. The hall is tiled—marble, but gritty with something like sand or salt. What had I been expecting? A wild terrain, a jungle?

I shiver, rubbing my arms to warm up. "They should turn up the heat up in here," I say.

"There is no 'they,'" he says.

"What is this place?" My whisper echoes as if I'd shouted.

"A museum."

We start walking down the hall. Our images double and triple, bouncing back and forth between the mirrors infinitely. The only sound is a distant rustling and ticking.

He turns down a hall with red carpeting, soaked like someone just hosed it down. I think of the cruise ship, but there are no panicked throngs of people, no one chasing us with guns.

We pass displays, not antiques, just outdated. One room is an ordinary living room, wall-to-wall carpeting, framed family photographs of people posing by old automobiles. There's an ordinary childhood bedroom with bunk beds and an ordinary kitchen, but cupcakes have been set out on the counter as if someone were just here.

Each room is cordoned off with a red velvet rope.

Jax starts walking faster.

"What kind of museum is this?" I ask, running after him.

"A life," he says.

"Whose life?" I ask.

"Your father's," he says. "But don't look. You can't get caught up in it all. I mean it. Keep passing them."

I do what he says, but then I glance into a room and find people, all completely stiff, as if made of wax. They're sitting around a dining room table, except for a little boy who's standing on his chair holding a tiny army man with a parachute—and I remember letting go of an army action figure off of a balcony, the parachute popping open and my father catching it, below. But this parachute looks hardened. The boy is smiling, frozen. Another boy about two years older is leaning over his plate, trying to get a better view.

There's a middle-aged mother and father. And then I recognize the father—Gemmy, just younger and trimmer. He's carving a turkey. His wife, my grandmother, sits at the other end of the table. I recognize her from an old photograph that my mother kept. She's smiling but looks teary-eyed. I look again at the two boys—Alex and Ellington, young, maybe eight and ten.

Jax runs back to me and slips his hand into mine. "We have to go," he says. "You can't let yourself get lost here."

"This was when they were just kids, maybe even still friends." I'm mesmerized. I can't look away. The dining room has a large window, casting them in afternoon light. I point at my grandmother's face. "She knows something is coming. See her expression."

"We have to keep going," Jax says.

I ignore him. "Are they made of wax?"

I step over the rope. I have to get a closer look.

An alarm sounds. I ignore it. There is no *they,* so there are no security guards.

I walk up to Gemmy. "He's so lifelike."

"Don't! We have to go!"

I touch Gemmy's shoulder expecting the firmness of wax, but it's warm and soft.

"I'm serious, Alicia. Come with me."

"I can't. I just want to be with them for just a minute."

And then Gemmy's eyes shift to meet mine.

I rear back. "Gemmy!" I shout. I turn to Jax. "He's alive!"

"No," he says. "He isn't. Not really. This world isn't like the world you know."

I look around the table.

All of their eyes turn to me, but they're frozen and quiet. There's still the sound of rustling, like something trapped and restless.

I steady myself by gripping the table. "Can we help them?" I ask Jax. "Can we save them?"

"They can't be saved. They exist in this form," he says. "We don't have much time."

I look out their dining room window. There's a light snowfall. So real and delicate.

What is this place?

"The atlas," Jax says, and he pulls me out of the room, over the rope.

We both start sprinting. The strange rustling and ticking grows louder. We pass classrooms and altars. Some of the rooms have fur-

niture covered in sheets. Some of them are just storage—boxes, old
refrigerators, stacks of photo albums, old bikes and sleds.

And then the ticking noise is right there. On either side of us are
rooms of bodies, wrapped in white plastic sheets, like cocoons. The
plastic is just pale enough that I can see their stiff physical forms but
not the details of their faces. And now I know where the noises are
coming from: each time their bodies flinch and shudder, the plastic makes noise.

Are they alive? Are they being preserved? They hang in their
wrapping, suspended from ceiling hooks that creak as the plastic
twists ever so slightly.

"Jesus," I whisper.

I imagine the hell of this world for my father—his life packed
up and weirdly preserved. The roots—how far do they go on? I created one. What's it like? Do I even want to know?

Jax says, "This way! We have to get there before the tide rolls
in."

"The tide?"

He throws his weight against a large door. "My mother said
there's an ocean nearby."

The door swings open onto a desert, sand in all directions.

And off to one side, there's a cliff.

At its edge, a house sits, sand pushed up against it like a snow-
drift. There's nothing else but sky—gray but lit up with diffuse sunlight, a bright fog.

"That's where they live," Jax says. The sand is applying so much
pressure that the house seems to be tilting over the cliff.

"Who?"

"Your parents," he says.

I look around at the barren landscape and back at the museum,
which now looks small and shrunken against the expanse of sky.

We head across the sand. The wind whips it up in small, quick whirlwinds. "How was this world made?"

"When your father decided between the prime where he stayed with your mother and the branch where she went back to Alex, there was a third subconscious choice. That's what the roots are for—what gets deeply buried, almost forgotten."

"And in this choice?" I say.

"Your father wanted everything to stay the same. No past, no future. Just the present. And this is how it showed up."

"My parents are in that house? The same age that they were on the day he made that decision?" I think of "Suicide off Egg Rock," when the man walks into the water at the end, how the surf is riding up on the ledges. "Yes."

I start to sprint across the sand to the house.

"Wait!" Jax shouts, following me.

The front door faces the cliff.

There's no way in.

The sand drift is deep. I start to climb it. I struggle to keep my footing. Finally I get to a window that's covered in sand. I dig so that I can see through the panes.

And there they are, asleep on a single mattress, my father's arm cradling my mother, his hand on her stomach, which is where I am—a collection of small cells.

They're so young—not that many years older than I am. It's crazy they were ever this young, much less in love and about to have a baby.

My father is shirtless. His tattoo isn't the complex tree that it is now. It doesn't even work its way down his arms or up his neck, just over his shoulder and down his back. My mother wears a T-shirt. The sheet is a tangle at their feet.

A television is on but only airs static. There's a broom by the door, but still the floor is sandy, with small piles swept into the corners of the room.

I raise my fist to knock on the window, but my mother's eyes open as if she senses something. She kisses my father's cheek. He smiles before he's even awake. They start talking, hushed whispers. I want to stay here and just watch what it would have been like—my parents, in love.

"Remember," Jax says. "They won't know you."

I'd forgotten this. Of course they won't know me. I haven't been born. "How will I get the atlas from them?"

"The atlas shouldn't mean much to them here. The past is a museum. I think the tide represents the future. Hard to say. It's not my subconscious. But I know it's hard to ignore the future. It keeps coming at you."

"What tide? You keep talking about a tide!"

He looks back over his shoulder. And now I see waves rippling up around the museum's sides, coming from some unseen ocean beyond it.

"Is it coming all the way here?" I ask.

"How do you think the sand gets pushed against the house?"

A wave crashes against the back of the museum, which seems small now, like a dollhouse from here.

I dig some more until I can grip the cross of the windowpane. I pull it up. Some sand trickles into the house, ticking against the floor like the inside of an hourglass.

I look back at the ocean. It pushes all the way around the museum meeting in front of it and rushing toward us before receding again.

The Plath poem is a whisper in my head, the part about the waves pulsing like hearts.

It's coming in fast.

I climb in the window. There's no place to hide an atlas in here. It's too bare.

I look at my father.

"Dad," I say, pushing on his shoulder.

My father's eyes open and he jolts up—as if he's used to waking to emergencies. He stares at me. He turns to my mother. "Francesca! Someone's here." But he hears the waves, not far off, and he starts to restack sandbags along the interior wall facing the tide.

My mother sits upright. "Who are you?"

"I'm your daughter," I say, quietly.

My father whips around, holding a sandbag in his arms about the size of a bundled baby.

My mother says, "I don't have—" But then she stops. "You're here from another . . ."

"I'm here for the atlas. I think you know what I mean." I look at my father. "Another you came down here and hid it."

If what I'm saying surprises my father, he doesn't react to it. He's too overwhelmed with me, my presence in this shack. He says, "Look at you." His voice is hushed and awed.

A wave splashes up against the window and pours in over the sill. It streams down the sandbags.

My mother stands up. The T-shirt is long. Her legs are bare. "You're beautiful," she says, smiling and suddenly crying at the same time. She puts a hand on her stomach. "We're waiting," she says.

"Are you waiting forever?" I ask. "Shouldn't you get out of here?" I turn to my father. "I could help get you out. I'm from the prime. I can—"

My father shakes his head. "This is our house. This is the world we live in. We chose it. It didn't lay claim on us."

He walks to the small table with two chairs and pulls one to the middle of the room. He climbs it, reaching up into the rafters.

Another wave hits. The house shivers.

I run to the window. "Jax! Are you okay?"

"I'm on the roof. I'm fine. But hurry!"

When I turn back, my father is holding something wrapped in tarp and knotted with twine. "This is it." He hands it to me. "Take it."

"Do you have any advice? About Alex, your brother?"

My father shakes his head, but my mother says, "He's a human being. Deep down, he wants the same thing as everyone else."

I'm about to tell her that Alex wants power. That's what he's always wanted. But then another wave hits the house. I glance back at the window. "I can get you out of here. This house is going to get pushed right off—"

My father grabs me and hugs me. My mother wraps her arms around both of us. We huddle like that for a moment—a family, a real family.

Then my father and mother let me go and cling to each other.

"Is there a better place out there for us?" she asks. "Is there a world where we stay together?"

I don't want to tell them the truth, but I have to. I shake my head. "No. I don't think so."

"You better go," my father says.

I want to stay. I want to burn their faces into my memory, but the waves are coming. I know I have to go.

I run to the window and climb out. "Thank you!" I shout.

My parents wave, then my mother lays her head on my father's chest.

I shut the window and climb up onto the roof just as another wave crashes into the house, like hitting the prow of ship.

Jax reaches out and steadies me, pulling me up. I can see the other side of the cliff. It opens into a dark hole, a gulf of nothingness. The thought of them crashing over the edge almost brings me to my knees. I want to crawl back in the window and drag them out.

"You got the atlas!" Jax shouts above the loud surf.

The wind whips around us. "Yes! Hold on to it and I'll hold on to you!"

He presses the atlas to his chest, and I wrap my arms around him. It feels good to hold him tight.

I push my fist into my collarbone, and just as I'm about to skin a knuckle against the roof, a wave pounds so hard that we're caught in a fine spray. The next wave might push us off the roof.

The water recedes, but I can see the next wave forming, like it's drawing in a deep breath quickly. It's like the ocean is speeding up.

Before I can do anything, the next wave pounds the house, slamming the roof. It rolls over us and we're soaked.

Then, before we can catch our breath, the next wave draws itself up, curling over our heads. Jax holds me as hard as he can, and I know this is the wave. This is the one. It pounds us, ripping us apart, and shoves us off of the roof.

Both of us, falling.

Still gripping the atlas, Jax is reaching for me.

And, as the wind tears all around us, I'm reaching for him.

Our hands touch.

I don't know what's below us. I see only white misty fog.

We grab hands. He reels me to his chest. "Just think of it! Use your imagination! See it!" he says.

I close my eyes tight, and as I imagine our bloody deaths, each fleck of water turns as red as blood, a sea of it. The red droplets tear mercifully away from the sky, the fog, the open gulf of air.

CHAPTER TWENTY-TWO

JAX AND I stare at each other, breathless. With one arm he's holding the package wrapped in tarp. The sun is hot, as if the atmosphere that holds it in check is being erased. The wall at my back gives a little, and some of it crumbles to the ground.

Now that I'm no longer in the roots, it's hard to imagine that the world of my father and mother living in a house on a cliff actually exists. If it doesn't, I'm suddenly scared that the package isn't an atlas at all. "I have to see it."

"Me too." Jax unknots the string, unwraps the tarp, and there it is.

The leather cover is stamped—branded, it seems, with the shape of a tree. Jax runs a finger along the grooves.

He flips open the cover. On the first page, there's an inscription: *We are one infinite tree in an infinite forest.*

We slowly turn the pages. Each one is filled with trees, with names, dates, the word that goes with their triggers, and a pressure point—letter-number combinations I remember from Hafeez's explanation of acupressure.

Some even have descriptions of the decisions that made the world—life or death, theft, war, love.

The trees remind me of my father's tattoos. Only magnified. And drawn in meticulous, mesmerizing detail.

"It's beautiful," I say.

"And dangerous," Jax reminds me.

The pages are a mix of cloth, leather, and paper as thin and soft as silk. The last pages look to be the oldest, written in crowded calligraphy, the ink in a language I can't understand.

Lodged in the back of the atlas against the leather binding, there are pages of dark, coiling shapes—some spiral in on themselves—covering the pages from edge to edge.

"The roots," Jax says.

Each page looks like it was added to over time. In some places the detail is hand drawn. In other places it's hand stitched, a glimmer of gold thread here and there.

The atlas is hypnotic. But I can't keep gazing at it. I push it back into his hands. "Take good care of it," I say.

"You want me to keep it?"

"Yes," I say. "It has to stay here."

He rewraps it. "If that other Alex really let all these people suffer and die—this whole world—then you can't give this to him. You can't. Even if we can save this world, he'd have access to all of these others. . . ."

"I'm going to use the atlas to lure Alex back with the new vaccine. My mother told me he wants what everybody else wants. I thought she meant power, but what if she really meant something else?"

"Like what?"

I'm too embarrassed to say the word "love," but then Jax says it for me. "She meant love. Didn't she?"

"I think so."

"You do what you have to do. I'll figure out a way to protect the atlas."

I have the holiday card and the phone-book page—hopefully enough to convince Alex to see this world for himself—and the photograph of Jane and Jax.

"I have to go," I say, but I don't want to. I know that when I jump, the other me will be here with Jax. I'm jealous of her. It's weird to be jealous of yourself. I can't leave though. I have to ask: "Jax?"

"What is it?"

"When I showed up, me, with Biddy sleeping in the room, you were going to tell me that you weren't interested in—"

"I wasn't talking to *you,* Alicia. Not *this* you."

"Oh. Okay. Good."

"Good?" he says, smiling.

"Yeah, good."

"Because if it had been you," he says and then he seems shy suddenly. "It would have been different. So hurry back, okay?"

"Okay." my pulse is fluttering.

I push on the bones of my hand and think of snow, light and powdery. The world flattens and pulls apart. The snow is blinding.

PART III
UNFURL

CHAPTER TWENTY-THREE

COLD WIND whipping all around me.

The roar of an engine.

I'm in the passenger seat of a speeding car. The top's down. I gasp and clutch at the dashboard with my free hand. I've got Jax's photograph, the Houston phone-book page, and the holiday card in my other hand. Quickly, I slip them under my jacket. Jane's driving. I'm wearing the clothes I had on the night I left the house with the gun. Jane must have busted me out of the hospital, or maybe she was just following orders. "Where the hell are we going?" I ask.

She looks at me sharply. "You're back then."

"Yes."

Jane shouts over the wind, "Where's the atlas? I thought you were closing in! Olsson said you were."

I rub my wrists, which are raw from the hospital bed cuffs. "I have a plan," I say. "Can we put the top up? I'm freezing."

She pulls over onto the crumbling shoulder, slaps on the flashing lights, and hits a button that makes the convertible top glide almost silently into place. Everything is suddenly quiet and still. The car's red leather interior and chrome glows. "What about Jax? Why isn't he with you?"

"He won't leave."

"What? Why not?"

"Why does it matter to you?" I say, wanting her to level with me.

She bangs her fist on the steering wheel, then grips it with both hands.

"Is this your car?" I ask. I thought I remembered a Subaru station wagon.

"It's a Maserati, a belated birthday gift from Alex for your sweet sixteen, assuming you can deliver for him, which I guess you can't."

"If he thinks he can buy my loyalty with a car, he's more of an idiot than I thought."

"Trust me," Jane says. "He's no idiot."

She pulls back into traffic. I've never seen her so agitated, weaving in and out of traffic way too fast. Maybe the news about Jax has shaken her—she looks close to tears.

"Did Olsson tell Alex to have the vaccine ready?"

"Yes. Alex has it. But how are you going to get him to hand it over?"

I hang on to my seat. "I have an offer for Alex," I tell her.

She changes lanes rapidly, from one to the other and back again. The speedometer quivers around ninety. "I hope, for your sake, it's a good one."

"Aren't you hoping for *your* sake, too, Jane?" She looks at me and then quickly away. "How's my dad?"

"He's still alive."

I'm so grateful, I almost start to cry. Overhead there's a dark blue night sky. The beach is off to the right. It reminds me of my parents' house on the cliff. "Where are you taking me?"

Jane pulls up at a red light. People in other cars stare at this beautiful machine we're sitting in and at us too: Who could be driving such a piece of art? I'm sure we're disappointing.

"Alex prefers to work deals away from the facility," she says.

The light turns green and she guns it.

I look out the window, pretending I feel calm and confident. "You don't even have a license to be a shrink, do you? All those books on terrible shit that people go through, lined up on your shelves—were they loaners?"

"Why would that even matter now that you know what you know?"

"Because you're still not telling me the whole truth! Why does that world matter so much to you, Jane?"

She stares ahead, jaw set.

I pull out the photograph. "Maybe because of this?"

Jane recognizes it immediately. "Where did you find that?" Her voice is shaky. "If Alex sees that—"

"Just so we're clear, we both have a lot at stake here. Jax isn't leaving that world, because he really wants to save it."

Her face pinches as if her son's name, spoken aloud, pains her. For the first time, I really see her as Jax's mother, and I feel her sorrow.

"He's the reason you got cut, right? That's why you told me that being a spandrel is a hard way to live."

She accelerates up the ramp onto I-93. The car slices the air. All the city is in front of us, lit up like Christmas. She shifts gears, speeding through traffic. Her eyes flood with tears, which then streak her cheeks. We drive on through the Tip O'Neill Tunnel. "I kept seeing all of the glimpses of his life with someone who wasn't me," she says. "It was so hard to see the life that you can't have playing out before your eyes, out of reach."

"But couldn't you go into that branch?"

"I'm not as good a spandrel as you and your father. I could only go in if your father piggybacked me, and I only did that once when Jax was little. But it was too disturbing to Jax—two identical mothers—and too dangerous. I couldn't risk anyone knowing."

And then we're out of the tunnel and on the streets of downtown Boston. The buildings tower over us.

"You mean Alex."

She nods. "I couldn't risk him being able to use Jax against me in any way. To use Jax at all. I'm sorry. You have to understand."

I do. She was trapped.

She's taking Cambridge Street, sliding through traffic, and then we come up to the glass walls of the Charles/MGH T station. She cuts across the intersection into a parking lot that looks like it's reserved for doctors who work at Mass General. She blows right past the empty guard booth; there's no one inside it now.

She pulls into a parking space. I don't know if we've arrived or if she's just collecting herself.

"His mother . . . the other you . . ." I don't know how to say what has to come next. How do you tell someone they're dead in another world?

"What?" Jane says.

"She's . . . gone."

"The virus?"

I nod. "Jax won't give up on the people left there. It's why I want the cure."

"I can't go on if he's gone," she whispers. She looks around the lot, like Pynch tracking takers. What is she watching for here? She takes a deep breath, checks her phone. "Let's go."

We both get out of the car and start walking. Across the street is a large gray building with a churchlike top. Behind it are huge hospital buildings.

We walk to the end of the parking lot. I can hear the rush of cars on Storrow Drive.

She stops at the edge of a crosswalk. "I have to leave you here."

"Here?" Here is nowhere in particular. "At a crosswalk?"

"I'm sorry." And I know she's trying to apologize for the danger she put me in, hoping to save her own son. "Look," she says, "if you can get Alex into that world and out of this one, Olsson and I have a plan to free your father."

"Alex isn't so different from anyone else, deep down. I think I can do it."

"We'll be ready."

"Wait." I hand her the photograph of her and Jax.

She touches it as if she could stroke Jax's cheek.

"It's yours," I say. She reaches out, holds it with both hands for a second. As she slips it carefully into her purse, I see a flicker of movement over her shoulder.

A man in a suit, face tilted down, talking on a cell phone on the opposite corner.

Another man, also in a suit, is leaning against a wall near a coffee shop.

A third man is looking down from the T platform.

All their faces are shadowed.

A hot shiver spreads through my chest.

"Jane," I say, and she looks up.

A woman in a thick coat and sunglasses is holding a small dog at the entrance to a construction site under the platform.

"Wait," I say. My fear is getting the better of me. "Where's Olsson? Jane, I think you should come with me. We should stick together and—"

She shakes her head. "Shh. Don't say anything more." And then she hugs me tight. I'm caught off guard. I don't want to hug her back, but I can't help it. I'm suddenly afraid I'll never see her again. "We'll be here for you when you get back," she whispers.

And then she lets me go, and as she walks back to the car, I see another figure, hanging out at a bus stop. This one is so tall and lanky I'd recognize him anywhere, Hafeez. Does Jane know he's here? Did he bully his way into getting a chance to help, or is he flying solo? Either way, I'm incredibly happy to see him, but I look away so I don't tip anyone off that he's here. I stand there, waiting, feeling alone but also watched, like the gazes are sliding over my skin.

And that's when I look up at the churchlike tower in front of me. I see the circular window—four large circles and then smaller ones fit in between, with one of the small windows in the center of it all.

The oculus.

The Liberty Hotel.

I look at all of the lit windows—floors and floors of them.

My father is in there.

I remember the view through that one small bit of curtains— the curved edge of the windows—and I try to match it with the windows in front of me. I start to count floors.

And then someone touches my elbow.

I spin, startled.

Sprowitz. Panic rolls through me so hard I'm almost nauseous.

"Come with me," he says. "Alex is waiting."

My legs are quivering. I can't speak. But I have to keep myself together.

We head toward the Liberty, his hand on the back of my arm, gripping me tightly.

The lobby of the Liberty Hotel is wide open with massive hanging circular light fixtures, people chatting on sofas—postures stiff, faces taut and shining—beautiful clerks and well-dressed doormen and, all around, stacked floors of hotel rooms. This place was once a prison?

And, high above it all, the oculus windows are glittering with the night sky behind them.

It smells like money—a perfumed chemical newness.

All the beauty and grandeur remind me of who I am and where I'm from—saggy chain-link fence, broken windows reinforced with cardboard, cars up on blocks. What if I'm just as flimsy as the house I grew up in? What if I can't do this?

We get to the elevators, but Sprowitz doesn't push a button. He just waits in front of one set of doors. They open.

We step inside.

The doors glide shut. He hits a button for the fourth floor.

"Does Alex have the vaccine?" I ask, though I'm pretty sure I shouldn't. "Is he going to free my father?"

"Shut up," Sprowitz says. A vein stands out on his neck, which is stubbled with razor burn. I look down at his wide knuckles. He looks like in another life he'd be a butcher in a blood-smeared apron.

The doors glide open. We step into the hallway.

"Aren't there guests around? Doesn't someone know what's going on?"

Sprowitz just laughs at me.

We walk down corridors and stop at a door. He knocks.

I'm bracing myself. Am I about to see my father—still strung up?

The door opens, and it's a fancy hotel suite—a bedroom off to the right with big fluffed pillows on the neatly made bed. And Alex, straight ahead, is sitting behind a desk.

One guard stands by the window, hands clasped, feet wide. He wears a crisp suit, and a wire snakes from one ear into his collar. And when he turns his head, I see a jagged scar on his cheek. And I recognize him immediately. This is the man who killed me in the cruise ship world. My murderer. Iosif.

I feel a strange fiery sensation spread through my chest.

My killer. In front of me. There's nothing I can do or say now.

Sprowitz takes his position by the other window, his face a blank stare.

Alex smiles at me—a weird, twisted smile that looks like it hurts. There's a small box on the desk in front of him and a bottle of champagne chilling in a glass bucket.

I can't believe how he fooled my mother all these years—sometimes even me—pretending to care so much about me. "What are we celebrating?" I ask.

"A minor breakthrough," he says. "Why don't you have a seat?" He points to a chair next to his massive desk.

"I'm fine," I say. I don't want to be ordered around under the guise of hospitality. "I'll stand." Just that one act of resistance has calmed me a little. I'm taking everything in. I focus on breathing evenly.

"Okay then," Alex says. He leans forward, elbows on the desk. "You know why I like this place?"

"Could it be the old-prison vibe?"

Alex smiles. "I'm sure you know that spandrels existed long before this was a prison, long before the ideas of physics and the multiverse, in fact. Way back, spandrels were shamans and spirit guides, or sometimes demonized. So, yes, a good number rotted away in this very prison, and not so very long ago. The worlds they made are still going. With the atlas, do you know how many worlds we'd have access to? All those family lines. Imagine!"

"This is all very interesting, but I'd like to know where my father is." I know he's in this hotel somewhere. I feel restless because I'm so close but can't save him.

"How about you tell me where the atlas is."

"I don't want to hand that over without being sure you have what I asked for."

Alex opens the lid of the box. A single slim vial sits in a groove inside its velvet lining. "This can be replicated in any lab. That's the beauty of it—cheap, high-volume." He puts the vial back and closes the box. He doesn't miss how my eyes follow it. "So why do you want to save that one world? Why so fixated?" He taps his fingers on the edge of the desk. "I mean, I understand why you'd want your father freed, but that world? Why not a fresh one?"

"Because in that world," I say, "you're my father."

The room is silent. Sprowitz and the other guard are completely still.

Minutes seem to pass before Alex stands up. "Get out," he says to the guards. "Give us our privacy."

They both leave and I almost wish they hadn't. They weren't on my side, but not having any witnesses is scarier.

Alex walks to the window. "Alicia," he says, smiling, "that's pretty hard to believe. I mean, you're saying your father created a world in which—"

"He did the right thing," I say. "At some point, he figured out you'd be the better husband and father. My mother went back to you."

He spreads his hand wide and flat against the pane of glass. "Then

I guess you know about my history with your mother." He doesn't look at me. I know his mind must be racing. "I know my brother." He stares out on the Charles River. "I'm sorry to say, but he's never done the right thing."

"Except in this case, he did."

"Your mother loved me once. You know that, right?" I know my mother never loved him. She had been trying to do the smart thing.

Alex pulls the curtain aside. "I thought that what he did had been so easy it never tore him up, not even for a second." Alex looks at me. His eyes are wild, like they're quivering. It's as if he's seeing the past run through his mind at a hyper-fast speed, again and again—lots of versions of it.

I pull out the holiday card with the picture of Alex, me, and my mother on the ski slope. "Their world is dying. You're killing it. There isn't much time." I put the card on the desk and slide it to him.

He picks it up and looks at it for a long time. He eyes it, hungrily. Finally, he lays the card gently down on his desk. "That's lovely. It really is. But how do I know it isn't fake?"

I pull out the page I tore from the Houston phone book, the one that lists "Alex and Francesca Maxwell." I hand it over. "How about this?"

Alex considers this piece of evidence a bit longer. "Well done," he says. "But my sources say otherwise."

"Did I really have time to fake two pieces of evidence *and* get the atlas?"

Alex picks up the box on his desk, walks around to me, and tilts the box toward me so I can see the viscous golden liquid. "You never really answered my question. Why don't you tell me what's in it for you—saving this world? It's not about me. Why's this one so precious?"

I can feel heat coming into my face. Alex thinks my father is dead in that world, and I can't let him know about Jax. "It's still one of my father's worlds. Broken as it is. He cared about it, and so do I. That's the thing. The people in these worlds are real. You and Jane told me for years they were just hallucinations, but they exist." This doesn't interest my uncle so I drive to the real point. "The atlas is in that world. So if you let that world die out, it goes, too. We'll make the exchange there. Nowhere else."

Alex raises his eyebrows. It's nice to surprise him for once. I swipe the holiday card off the desk to give him another look. "It's ironic. You attack the one world that has the life you really wanted. Don't you want to at least see it before it's gone?"

"I'm not so sure I believe you have the atlas."

"But once you see it, will you agree?—the atlas for the vial and my dad's freedom?"

Alex is staring at me, thinking it over, and then he cocks his head. "Sometimes you look just like your father. It's amazing, the resemblance."

He brushes his hand through his hair, and it's clearly shaking. He walks back around the desk, opens the top drawer. He pulls out a gun and twists it in the air. "Remember this little beauty? You know I gave it to your mother as a gift one Christmas. A woman alone with her young daughter in a house should protect herself from intruders, right?"

"You don't need a gun," I say.

"The gun's a deal breaker for me. If the vaccine comes, so does the gun.

"Fine. I can take you in," I say. "Let's go."

"You think I'd travel with a novice?" Alex walks to the door. I hear him talking to someone in the hallway.

He returns with Sprowitz. He can piggyback?

"Your gift is rare," Alex says, "but I collect rarities."

Sprowitz tries to smile, as if being part of one of Alex's collections is an honor.

Alex still has the box tucked in one jacket pocket and the gun in a holster that runs across his back. "We know your father's mind trigger. Blood. And this world is . . . where?" He seems to search his memory.

"Collarbone."

"Yes."

Alex looks at Sprowitz, who gives a nod. He's ready.

Now I only have to think of blood, and the flash in my head is my uncle's blood, spilling on the floor. It's that fast—red behind my eyes. Do I really want him dead?

I push my knuckle into my clavicle. The red in front of my eyes recedes. The room stretches thin.

And the last thing I see is Alex's face pulled to one side like it's made of elastic, then snapping.

And in less than a second, but what feels stretched into hours in the hurtling dark, I hear Sprowitz's voice. "Remember when we were kids," he says. His voice is different, shy almost. It fills my ears while my eyes only see shadows and feel the rush of air around me. "In that Florida motel," he says, "watching lizards hunt moths on the window screen?" His voice seems to have no body. It's a voice that exists almost in my own mind. But it's clearly his.

No, I think. *No, I don't remember anything about us as kids,* but my mind rockets, trying to understand what he means.

And then I see it—orange nubby bedspreads, lamplight, Sprowitz and I are maybe ten years old, on our bellies crosswise on the bed nearest the window, staring into the dark humid night. The family bosses had met up. Sprowitz and I were left to entertain ourselves.

"The thing is, I rooted for the lizards," he says, his voice like a wind dragging past me. "I was drawn to them because they were lean and strong and hungry. But you always rooted for the moths, who seemed to know when the lizards were coming. They could feel the vibrations of the screen. Sometimes you'd flick the screen to warn them."

I remember how it felt to flick the screen, how relieved I was when the moths flitted away.

"I think I picked the wrong side," Sprowitz whispers.

Now I see splotches of light and dark. His voice is gone. There's no wind now, no sound.

CHAPTER TWENTY-FOUR

AND THEN from nowhere, the feeling of solid surface under my feet.

Alex is doubled over, coughing, but still clutching the small box that holds the vaccine. Sprowitz is lying on the floor, his heavy shoulders shuddering. I look at him, wondering if he'll acknowledge what he said to me. I know Alex didn't hear it. Sprowitz meant it only for me. But he won't look at me. He won't make eye contact.

I'm standing by the front door of my house in this world. Two long thin windows let in brittle light on either side of the door. Hopefully back in the prime, Olsson is meeting up with Jane, getting ready to break my father out. I push back a curtain—so delicate and worn that it disintegrates in my hand. I touch the window, and it bows out like warm plastic.

We must have connected with Pynch, where he said he would circle back, and he's brought Jax and me—this me—back from Houston. I know there's a plan, but it's hazy and fragile, more like the feeling of hope.

The sun is brighter than ever, but it's as if it casts no warmth. In the street, a group of people are huddled around an old metal trashcan where someone's started a fire to keep warm. I'm assuming they're here to help in some way. Maybe as backup if this gets physical.

I look for Jax. One face turns toward me. It's Pynch, holding his hands over the flames. He bobs his head and turns back to the fire quickly.

Is he here to help? Are the others also from the camp? This is part of Jax's plan; I'm sure of it, but I just wish my brain could dredge up the rest of the details.

I can sense my mother upstairs, still hanging on. Alex has piggybacked in. His other self could be somewhere in this house.

"Where is the atlas?" Alex says, still wheezing.

"It's here. It's coming," I say. "I swear."

Sprowitz leans against the wall, taking everything in, trying to get his bearings. "Nice place," he mutters, and I can see the boy he was, his light freckles, his quick eyes, his fine feathery hair. We were friends once, and then Alex must have come along, made him an offer.

Alex lurches into the living room. "Jesus," he says.

He's found the family portrait—Alex, Francesca, and a young version of myself in my lace collar and neatly trimmed bangs. "It's real." He turns a slow circle, taking in the room—its weak and cracking walls, the ribboned curtains. Down feathers have escaped the sofa pillows and spin in a draft.

Alex's eyes start to well up. I've never seen him cry. He shouts at Sprowitz: "Get out of here! Stand by the door!"

Sprowitz gives me a quick look—a moment of embarrassment or helplessness, almost like he doesn't want to leave me alone with my uncle, but he excuses himself and opens a door to bright, glaring light, then closes it behind him.

I wish Sprowitz had stayed, even though he'd never help me. Or would he? If he rooted for the moths and not the lizards?

"She's here," Alex whispers. He means my mother. "Where? Where is she?"

What did I expect? Of course he wants to see her. Maybe he wants to know what it's like for her to look at him like she loves him. Does she love him in this world?

He rushes past the dining room and kitchen, then heads for the stairs, dust gusting into the air with each footfall.

"Wait," I say. "She's very sick." I run after him, feeling the puttylike give of the stairs under my feet. How long does this world have? Will there be enough time to bring those on the brink back? My mother—if I can get the vial, can she be saved?

By the time I get to my mother's room, Alex is kneeling beside her bed. The other Alex isn't here. His golf club leans against the armchair, the pile of newspapers stacked beside it on the floor.

The glow through the sheers is intense, but I can see the thin steam of my mother's shallow breaths in the cold air. She's propped with pillows, eyes closed. Her hair has been brushed back from her face. The monitor on the IV tree hooked to the battery pack beeps every few seconds.

Alex puts his hand on top of hers. "We can get her out of here," he says. "You can piggyback her into the prime, and we can start the new meds. She'll have a better chance, and when she pulls through—"

"You can't turn your back on all of these people just to save her," I say. Not to mention the tricky point that my mother exists in the prime. I guess Alex wants the one he can save and claim as his own.

"Don't tell me what I should and shouldn't do. Do you know how long I've waited for this? And it was here, god damn it. It was here all along."

And then my mother's weak eyes flutter open.

"Hey," Alex says. "You're going to be okay. I'm here. I'm right here."

She smiles a little, then frowns, confused. She must sense the difference.

"You should rest," Alex says. "You should sleep. We're going to take you to a facility that can—"

"You can't piggyback her. It could kill her," I say.

"Alicia," my mother whispers.

I walk to the foot of her bed. "I'm right here."

And then there's a voice downstairs. "Is everything okay? Alicia!"

Alex straightens. He knows the voice better than anyone—it's his own. Alex looks at me coldly. "Stay here with her. I'll take care of him."

"Wait," I say. "The atlas, the vaccine. We're here for an exchange. We're here to set this right."

Alex cuffs the back of my head and roughly pulls my face in close. "I could slip into this life."

"What life? There's no life here. It's falling apart!"

He lets me go and looks past me. His eyes are steely and fixed. He walks out of the room, and his hand slips under his jacket where the gun rests in its holster.

I scan the room before hastily grabbing the golf club. "I'll be right back," I tell my mother. "It'll be okay."

"No," my mother says. "Let him go!"

Does she know that she's talking about two Alexes? Has she been waiting for something like this to happen? "I have to," I say.

Her narrow chest rises and falls as she struggles to breathe. "Alicia," she says, but it's like she recognizes me—the real me, not her privileged daughter who grew up in a fancy house, but me, the one from Southie, the one who grew up with a single mom in a row house.

"I can do this," I tell her, and I mean me—this Alicia can do this. I run out the door and downstairs, hoping for a second that the Alex of this world kills Alex from the prime. It's a sickening thought and hopeless too. Alex of this world is tired and beaten down, weak and unarmed. And he's not the same man. He's not a killer.

When I get halfway down the stairs, prime Alex is pointing a gun—the gun he'd given my mother—at Alex of this world.

Alex of this world doesn't lift his hands over his head. He stands there, blank, emptied, too shocked to move. But there's something about him that seems to accept this, as if it were inevitable that some other version of himself might show up and pull a gun on him.

He notices me and gives me a sad look, and I can't help but wonder if he's always known—or had a strong suspicion—that I wasn't really his daughter, not in this world, not in any world. I squeeze the golf club, hoping he knows I grabbed it to defend him. But prime Alex turns the gun on me.

"Don't move or I'll blow both of you away. You hear me?"

"Stay where you are, Alicia," Alex of this world says to me gently. "This is just between me and him." And I know that he's always been a kind father to me—a good, loving one.

"So did you love your life here?" prime Alex asks.

"Yes. But the last couple years have been brutal," Alex of this world says.

"I want to know what it's been like. With her. Here. All these years."

"She made me a better man," Alex of this world says. "She never loved me the way she loved Ellington. But she was good to me." He looks at me. "To us."

Prime Alex squeezes the trigger; the gun pumps a shock through his arm, and he lets out a small grunt. I feel the vibration of the gunshot in my own ribs. Alex of this world falls, grabbing his shoulder. Blood seeps across his shirt.

My mother screams from upstairs, ragged and hoarse. I'm frozen. I don't know what to do except try to keep her up there. "It's okay. Just please stay where you are!"

Prime Alex moves in closer, stands over Alex of this world, who's shaking on the floor, breath jagged. It's as if he wants to watch himself slowly die. Was it the goodness that set him off? Or the fact that my mother couldn't ever love him here either?

A wash of blood from Alex of this world is spreading across the floor, which sends a shock of aches shooting through my body— my father's worlds calling me out of this one, all of those escapes— but I'm not going anywhere.

Prime Alex is so enthralled with the suffering that he's let down his guard. This is my chance. I grip the golf club, sidle a couple of steps closer, then wind up and crack the golf club across his backbone. Prime Alex arches, the gun clatters to the wood floor—a puff of dust swelling around it—and he falls to his knees.

The gun is out of his reach.

We both glance at it.

I raise the golf club over my head, ready to swing again, but he scrambles up, and before I can strike him again, he tackles me, pins me to the floor, and wrestles the golf club so both of us are holding it tight. He presses the cold metal of the club against my windpipe. I push against it, fighting for each breath.

Out of the corner of my eye, I see Alex of this world roll to his side and then his belly. He drags himself toward the gun. In this world he is still my father. He would do anything for me, I know this.

"The atlas . . ." I grunt to my uncle. "All those worlds. Remember?"

Alex could easily kill me but he just steadily keeps up the pressure so I can't really breathe. My mind dulls from lack of oxygen. "Can you imagine what it's been like to watch your shitty little childhood play out?" he says. "I've seen signs, all along. I knew you'd have all your father's gifts. I called it when you were just a toddler. You had everything I didn't."

I could tell him I was always just a piece of shit—another screwed-up Southie kid, but that isn't true. That's what Alex has gotten wrong all these years. It's not being a spandrel that made something of me. Through a strangled breath, I manage to say, "No, that's not–"

"I'm going to take you out," Alex says. "World after world."

Then, just as my vision starts to narrow to a bead of light and I'm about to pass out, I hear, "Not in this world."

But it's too late. Prime Alex rolls off of me, whips around, snatches up the gun before Alex of this world can get a clearer shot at him. Prime Alex points the gun directly at me. He pulls the box from his pocket. "Get me the atlas." He pops the box open, and, pressing it against his chest, he pulls out the vial. He holds it in the air, gripping it so tightly that his fist shakes. He drops the box. It hits the floor, sending out cracks across the marble. "Get it now!"

I look to Alex of this world. His eyes are fluttering shut, his breathing shallow. I hope that Jax is out there with a plan.

"Okay," I say. "Someone's brought it here for you."

Alex nods, almost imperceptibly, twitches the gun to the door to indicate where he wants me to go. The room feels like it could blow apart, billions of tiny pieces spinning loose.

I walk to the front door and open it.

The light is blinding at first—a sheer, bright pang when it hits my eyes.

But as they adjust, I see Jax standing in the street. Behind him, the crowd huddles around the fire in the metal can, black smoke billowing. Their bodies are hunched over the flame. All I can hear is the hiss of the fire and the wind.

Jax sees Alex right behind me. I put my hands up so he knows I have a gun shoved into my back. Pynch stands beside Jax, and for a moment I imagine them on the basketball team, waiting for the bus to take them to an away game, doing the things that maybe they should have, if things hadn't turned out this way.

Jax steps forward, chin up, gives Alex a defiant glare. "We have the atlas," he says. "Now, give us the vaccine."

"Let me see it first," Alex says. I can feel the gun in my back.

Jax pulls the atlas out from under his coat and backs slowly toward the metal can. He holds it up, stretching toward the fire. Its gold-stitched cover glows over the flame. "Give us the vaccine, or I burn this now," Jax says. His voice doesn't even tremble.

"Who the hell are you?" Alex says. He shoves me forward, levels the gun at Jax now.

"Don't!" I say, terrified. "Don't shoot!"

The little group of people run off.

"Freeze!" Alex screams. He points the gun at me but addresses the crowd. "You're all my hostages. Sprowitz!"

Sprowitz is standing on what used to be the front yard—now just dirt packed and cracking. He levels his weapon on the crowd. "No one move!" he shouts, shifting his weight and then taking a wide stance. He's trying to look tough, but there's something about him that makes him seem like he's already broken. His eyes catch mine for just a second, and I can tell he's scared.

Everyone stops. Everything is still, except the wind and the shifting and ticking of this disintegrating world.

Alex lifts the vial. It glints in the sharp sun.

"Vaccine first," Jax says to Alex.

He waves the atlas over the flame.

Alex smiles.

Before anyone can register what he's doing, he tosses the vial high in the air. It glitters in the harsh light as it flips end over end.

I jump down the front steps, keeping my eyes on it, running, trying to get under it. My feet pound, my hands reaching, and the vial turning. I'm sprinting across the lawn, and I throw myself forward. The ground races to meet me; the impact knocks my breath away.

Rolling in the brittle grass, I have the vial, warm in my hand. I can't believe it. I turn to Pynch to show him, and I see Alex rushing Jax, the gun trained at his chest.

Jax lowers the atlas toward the fire; the smoke billows around it.

"Give it to him!" I yell, but it's too late—he lets it go and the fire leaps up.

Then there's the tearing explosion of a gunshot, and Jax staggers backward and falls.

I push the vial to Pynch's chest and run to Jax.

Sprowitz is shouting for people to shut up, but it's chaos now. Everyone's running.

Before I can get to Jax, Alex grabs my arm and yanks me back so hard that my shoulder bangs into his chest.

He takes a few heavy steps, gripping my arm like he wants to tear it off. I struggle but I can't get free of him.

"Why did you do it?" I shout.

His head bobs side to side. He coughs and turns, spitting blood. "I didn't shoot. Someone shot me," he says.

I pull back just enough to see an imprint of blood from his shirt on my own.

"You," he whispers. "You did this to me."

"No," I said. "This is all you. You did this."

Alex whispers through his blood-smeared teeth. "Sprowitz!" he screams, his eyes squeezing shut. "See what she's done to me?"

Sprowitz lumbers to him just as Alex falls to one knee. Tears are streaming down Sprowitz's face. "I'm sorry," he says to Alex.

The gun falls from Alex's hand to the hard dirt. He kneels as if he's praying but then slouches backward.

"You?" Alex says to Sprowitz, and then he reaches up and touches Sprowitz's face.

Sprowitz's face is red, contorted. "I'm sorry," he whispers.

I take a step back, unable to look away as Alex draws in a gasp, his cheeks shuddering. He tightens his jaw and seems to look up at the sky, and then at nothing at all.

Sprowitz sobs so loudly that the cords stand out on his neck. And then he blinks, sits back on his heels. He pushes himself to his feet, wiping his eyes.

I back away from him, tripping.

The ground seems to tilt. My ears are ringing.

The fire, stoked by the atlas, pours black smoke across the yard. I run to Jax, drop to my knees beside him. His eyes are closed but fluttering. There's no blood. Alex didn't shoot him. Alex was the one who got shot.

I grab Jax's sleeve. "Are you okay?"

He squints and nods.

"I was so scared that you were gone," I tell him. "Tell me you're okay. Tell me again."

He cups my face in his palms. "The atlas," he says.

"It's all right," I say. "It doesn't matter."

"No," he says. "I faded out because I created a branch. The atlas is safe. The decision to burn it—I felt the tearing inside me. Everything split in two."

"You created another branch?"

Jax smiles. "And in that branch, you caught the vaccine, too."

Pynch walks up, lifts his hand, and there it is—golden and bright in the sun. He gives it to Jax.

"My uncle," I say to Pynch, "the one from this world. He's in the house. I don't know if he's still alive. And my mother, they need help. Can you . . ."

"I've got it," Pynch says, and then he strides toward house.

Jax closes his eyes, the lids tremble. Then he opens them and looks up at me. "I can still sort of see it, the branch I made."

I think of that new world, spinning out on its own. I want to stay here with Jax but I know I can't stay. People are moving through the thick smoke and bright sun. "I need to—"

"Go back." He sits up.

"My father . . ."

"I know."

"I don't want to leave you here," I say. "This world is—"

"About to be saved," Jax finishes for me. "We'll see each other again. I'll always know which version is you."

I help him stand and he pulls me in close, runs the back of his hand down my cheek and kisses me; it's warm and sweet, and I don't want it to end.

Finally, he pulls away from me, smiling, then turns and starts walking toward the truck. People are bustling through the wind-kicked veils of smoke.

Prime Alex stares vacantly at the sky, his skin waxy, his lips tinged blue.

And then through the smoke, I see Sprowitz. His eyes are full of tears—like he's terrified and angry all at once. The pistol dangles from his hand.

I take a few steps toward him. "Sprowitz?" I say. "Brian?"

He looks at me, then at the pistol in his hand. I freeze, feeling as if he could turn on me. But he holsters the gun and looks back up at me again. His eyes are glassy, unfocused, and he staggers a bit to one side. I wonder if he, like Jax, branched when he shot Alex.

"Did you?"

Sprowitz looks me. "Did I what? You saw me."

"No. I mean, was it a hard decision?"

He looks up at the ribboned sky and closes his eyes against the sun. "No," he says. "It wasn't. I didn't branch. That means there's something wrong with me, right?"

"No," I say. I reach out and touch his arm. "You saved our lives. Thank you."

"I looked at that book by that poet you like. Just so I'd know, you know, what you were thinking, what was in your head. One was written to a kid without a dad."

I'm trying to imagine Sprowitz reading a book for any reason, not to mention checking out Plath. "I know that poem," I say.

Sprowitz glances at me.

"It's about something growing beside you but an absence."

"A death tree," Sprowitz says.

"One without any color."

"She uses the words that spandrels use," Sprowitz says. "It was like she was talking right to me. To us, maybe. My father was a death tree for me all my life. Alex saved me."

"He used you."

"All this time I thought you were an idiot for not taking what he was ready to give you. Everything," Sprowitz says. "He'd have treated you like his own. Me? I had to earn it. But he'd have *given* it all to you, Alicia."

"You don't believe that, do you? Not anymore. You can't."

"No," he says. "Not anymore. You and I go way back." Alex's

orders were to give you a hard time. I never wanted to. Our fathers were friends but then mine died. And then Alex came along. Don't you remember now? A little?"

And I do. He's at my birthday parties; we're swimming at a lake; we're fighting at a dinner table; we're dividing Halloween candy. "It's the strangest feeling," I tell him, "but I miss that little boy named Brian Sprowitz."

He smiles, but only for a second. And then he's back to himself, gruff and loud. "We have to get out of here. There's a plan to get your father out."

I look for Jax and see him talking to Pynch, who's in his truck with a band of people in the back. I see Jax's face. His mouth is moving but I can't hear him.

I know I'll be back.

"Go on," Sprowitz says, handing me my father's gift, the tool. "They need you."

I take it, feel the nice fit of the handle in my palm. "Thanks."

Sprowitz doesn't say you're welcome. He walks off.

The air feels full of a fine dust, which flits around like powder. My hand starts to buzz, deep within it. I clasp my hands together, the tool locked into place, and I bear down.

It happens fast.

The world peels back, rolls in on itself, and is gone.

CHAPTER TWENTY-FIVE

I'M RUNNING up a set of stairs toward a fire door, my heart rocketing in my chest. I'm alive. I'm in the Liberty Hotel. And I'm running to find my father. I don't know if Olsson or Jane have held up their end of the bargain. I don't know where Hafeez is. Everything is a blur, and the only thing in my mind is that my uncle is dead. I whisper, "He's dead. He's gone," to no one, a light echo in the stairwell. It's just starting to sink in. I feel guilty but I tell myself not to. "He was going to kill Jax. It's not my fault." I remember Jax's eyes fluttering open, the warmth of his lips on mine. It's all so much to take in. It happened so fast, I'm reeling.

But I can't think of those things now. I'm taking the next flight, pounding up the stairs as fast as I can.

The door at the top of the stairs swings open.

There's Olsson, holding up my father, who's dressed in a T-shirt and jeans, barefoot. He looks like hell—eyes swollen to slits, lips so puffed they're split and blood crusted.

And now, as if they've just sprung loose, memories rush at me—warm washcloths, lunch boxes, Christmas mornings, piñatas, loud sing-alongs in the car, sledding, swimming, first days of school, picture-day dresses, bad haircuts, recitals, a clarinet. My father is there in all of them, hand on my shoulder, bending down to explain something. My father loves me; he always has. My father never jumped from world to world just to avoid living. He jumped in order to live more fully. He didn't destroy worlds. He tried to protect the ones he'd created.

"I'm here," I say, and I run up the last few steps to my father. I slip under his free arm and help prop him up.

"Okay, let's take it easy on the stairs. Jane's pulling the car around," Olsson says.

"Is that the plan?" I ask. "I mean, I'm here. It's *me*. I'm really here."

My father's silent. He squeezes my shoulder. It feels good—reassuring, a comfort.

"The atlas?" Olsson asks.

"It's safe—in another world. For now at least. Jax has the vaccine. They're going to try to save that branch."

My father can hardly hold his head up, but he smiles.

"And there's something else I have to tell you," I say. "Alex is dead. The one from the prime."

"Dead?" Olsson says.

"Sprowitz killed him."

Olsson and my father exchange looks.

"Iosif is going to try to take over," Olsson says. "He'll sense a vacuum of power and he'll move in."

"Iosif?" I say. "He's the guy who killed me. This isn't good."

"It's okay, Alicia," my father says. "It's going to be fine."

"Don't lie to her," Olsson says.

We get to the bottom of the stairs, and my father takes me by the shoulders. "You did good," he says. "Real good."

Olsson pulls open the door leading to a parking garage.

There's the Maserati. Jane steps out of the driver's door, runs to us. "Is Jax safe?"

"Yeah," I tell her. "He's fine."

Jane tightens her lips and then smiles. Her eyes tear up. "Thank you."

"I have a favor to ask," I say to Jane.

"Anything."

"You have to tell my mother I'm fine. I promise I'll call her, but I have to go figure out who I really am, and I can't do that in my old life."

"I'll tell her."

Olsson eases my father into the passenger seat. "Okay, you should head to New Bedford. There's a little airport there. The pilot will take you to a safe house. We'll have medical folks there who can help. Eventually, we'll get a world secured for you. Somewhere safe."

Jane hands me a set of keys.

"For this car?" I ask. "I'm driving? I'm only fifteen."

"Well, your father's in no shape to drive," Olsson says. "So—"

"No," Jane says, interrupting. "I found a driver."

From the cramped backseat, Hafeez emerges. He steps out of the car and I rush him, giving him a huge hug.

"He showed up at my house," Jane says. "He demanded to help."

"Where else could I go?" Hafeez says.

I introduce him to my father. My father's hands are too beaten to shake. Hafeez says, "I've heard a lot about you. Nice to meet you in person."

My father smiles. "Any friend of Alicia's is a friend of mine."

I hand Hafeez the keys and climb in the back.

"Good luck," Olsson says.

"We'll see you again soon," Jane says.

"Thank you," my father says to them.

Olsson and Jane nod and walk away, down the row of parked cars. I expect them to look back but they don't. Shoulders hunched to the cold, they just keep going, moving fast. At the end of the row, they split away from each other.

"You two ready?" Hafeez asks, gripping the wheel.

"Absolutely," I say.

He steps on the gas and the car pops forward and then takes off. "It's like flying," Hafeez says.

"Sure is," my father says.

CHAPTER TWENTY-SIX

A FEW weeks later, I'm in my father's bedroom in an old farmhouse surrounded by fields of tall wheat. I spend a lot of time sitting in this chair pulled to his bed. He's still wrapped in bandages, casts, but he's on the mend.

This is home for now. It's where we landed that night when my father was set free, on a rough strip of grass. A doctor and a nurse were waiting for him and tend to him, here, off the grid. Where is here exactly? Where's anywhere, really?

The house belongs to spandrels from the old family lines, ones that date back to the earliest known civilizations. On the bedside table are an old rotary phone, a comb, and a tool, the one my father gave me for my birthday.

Some nights, after my father has fallen asleep, like he has now, I call Hafeez when I know his mother's going to be out playing Bunco.

Some nights, I call my mother and we talk. Sometimes we talk about real things, the truth.

Some nights, I find myself writing down the Sylvia Plath lines that I love and have memorized. I doodle around and through the words with sketches of trees with branches and roots curling and spiraling out in all directions. I think of Sylvia as a spandrel, and how maybe, when she made the decision to kill herself, her world ripped in two. In one of them, she got up off the kitchen floor, struggled to her feet, closed the oven door, and turned off the gas. Covering her mouth with both hands, she walked up the stairs to her children's bedroom door. She peeled off the masking tape, pulled away the towels she'd put in place to protect them. In the small room, there was the milk and bread she'd left, the window yawning open for airing. The way I listen to my father breathing, she listened to the soft purring of her children's breaths, and she fell asleep, knowing that the next day, she'd keep going.

Some nights, I think about how we all just keep going—for ourselves and for each other, in universe after universe. In branch after branch. In the infinite forest. It makes me feel small but also as if each moment of each of our lives is vast, so full of unknowable things.

Outside, there's the rise and fall of cricket noise. Occasionally a pair of headlights will glide along the distant road.

I look out at the moon, a harvest moon—full and blushing.

A red moon.

A blood moon, some people call it.

I pick up the tool. It feels good and right in my hand, a relief.

I stare at the moon. The pain doesn't feel like pain anymore. It feels known, predictable. I press the tip of the tool on a specific spot on my arm first.

The crickets roar in my ears. The room spins so quickly that it feels like I'm inside of a tornado. The wallpaper, covered in flowers, seems to bloom and burst with color and then . . .

———

I'm up late, sitting on the porch of the cabin in a rocking chair. I'm looking out at the lake with the little girl with the bright green eyes—her name is Helen—asleep on my lap. Inside, I hear Gemmy laughing and talking. "Ticky-hi," I sing to her: "Ticky hi, ticky ho. Ticky hi-dy hi-dy ho. . . ."

I push back as I rock so that my lower ribs hit the slats of the rocker. The glinting off the lake looks like stars. I hear a coyote, and it howls, loud and sharp, in my ears. . . .

I'm sitting on a rooftop. Hafeez has his arm around me. Pixie Stix wrappers are lying on the shingles. Through the window, I see our backpacks, side by side on the floor. There's a little chill in the air. We're far from home. We left, together. I wouldn't get cut. I had to run. Hafeez didn't let me go alone.

I'm happy. And although I can't really exactly place where we're living, I can tell that in this world I'm exactly where I need to be.

"Big dipper," Hafeez says, pointing to the constellation.

We both are looking up now, and he taps his chest three times. The sign—the heart like in the Plath poem about the "red bell-bloom, in distress." I glance at him and then tap my own chest, right over my heart. He smiles.

I push my knuckle against my collarbone. I don't want to hang around. I just wanted to check in.

I look up at the stars, and they start to tremble and then bounce. The chill turns into a sharp wind. . . .

A vast dark blue sky. Far off, there's a line of people under the glow of lanterns, waiting in front of a medical tent. Sprowitz and Pynch are there, handing out supplies.

And Jax is beside me.

I hear a strange soft scratching. It seems to be coming from the ground itself.

I kneel down and put my palm flat on the dirt.

Jax turns and looks at me. "You?" he says.

I nod, and then I start to feel it, a needling sensation like my hand was asleep but is tingling with blood and nerves—the earth stitching itself together. "You have to feel this," I say to Jax.

He puts his hand on the ground, too. He looks up at me. "It's starting. It's because we all have a new way of perceiving the future."

"With a little hope."

He covers my hand with his. "What now?" he says.

But he must know the answer.

Everything.

Dear Reader,

J. Q. Coyle is the joint pen name of two authors, Quinn Dalton and Julianna Baggott. We met in graduate school, both aspiring fiction writers. Over the years, we've published many books. Quinn is an acclaimed writer who has published two short-story collections and two novels, most recently *Midnight Bowling*. Julianna has published more than twenty books, including *Pure*, a *New York Times* Notable Book of the Year (2012). Julianna came up with the concept behind the lives of spandrels, but really wanted to put two minds to the limitless possibilities of the idea itself. She reached out to Quinn and, together, they wrote the novel, back and forth, over many years. The result of those two minds cross-pollinating is now in your hands.

Sincerely,
J & Q